Witch's Business

Diana Wynne Jones

❖

Witch's Business

GREENWILLOW BOOKS

An Imprint of HarperCollins*Publishers*

First published in 1973 in Great Britain by Macmillan London Ltd.
under the title *Wilkins' Tooth*.
First published in 1974 in the United States by E. P. Dutton & Co.
under the title *Witch's Business*.
Reissued in 2002 by Greenwillow Books, an imprint of HarperCollins
Publishers.

The text of this book is set in Adobe Caslon.

Library of Congress Cataloging-in-Publication Data
Jones, Diana Wynne.
Witch's business / by Diana Wynne Jones.
    p.   cm.
"Greenwillow Books."
Originally published under title: Wilkins' tooth. Great Britain: Macmillan
London, 1973. Witch's business first published in U.S.: New York :
E. P. Dutton, 1974.
Summary: Frank and Jess's scheme to earn money by hiring themselves
out as revenge seekers seems like a good one until they discover they are in
competition with a witch.
ISBN 0-06-008782-X (trade). ISBN 0-06-008783-8 (lib. bdg.)
[1. Magic—Fiction. 2. Witches—Fiction. 3. England—Fiction.]
I. Title.   PZ7 .J684 Wk 2002   [Fic]—dc21   2002016170

10 9 8 7 6 5 4 3 2 1

For Jessica Frances

One

Frank and Jess thought Own Back Ltd. was an excellent idea when they first invented it. Three days later, they were not so sure. The trouble was that they were desperate for money. They had broken a new chair and all pocket money was stopped until the summer. They had to face four penniless months and, somehow, as soon as they knew this, they found all sorts of things they could not possibly do without.

"I can't go *anywhere*," said Jess. "The other girls expect you to pay your share. It isn't fair. Just because it was such a badly made chair. The other chairs turn upside down without breaking. I don't see why this one had to go and fall to pieces."

"Nor do I," said Frank, who was worse off than Jess. "I owe Buster Knell ten pence."

"Why?" said Jess.

"A bet," Frank answered. Jess was sorry for him, because Buster Knell was not the boy you owed anything if you could help it. He had a gang. Frank, in fact, was desperate enough to go down to the newsagent and ask Mr. Prodger if he wanted another boy for the paper route. But Mr. Prodger said Vernon Wilkins was all he needed and, besides, Vernon needed the money.

So Frank came dismally home and, after some thought, he and Jess put up a notice on the front gate, saying ERRANDS RUN. It had been up half an hour when their father came home and took it down. "As if you two haven't done enough already," he said, "without decorating the gate with this. When I said no money, I meant no money. Don't think I'm going to let you get away with immoral earnings, because I'm not."

It was the talk of immoral earnings that gave them the idea.

"I say," said Jess. "Do people pay you to do bad things for them?"

"If they want them done enough, I suppose," Frank

answered. "If it's something they don't dare do themselves, like pull Buster Knell's nose for him."

"Would they pay us?" said Jess. "If we were to offer to do things they didn't dare do?"

"Like what?" said Frank. "I don't dare pull Buster Knell's nose, either."

"No. More cunning than that," said Jess. "Suppose someone came and said to us: 'I want something dreadful to happen to Buster Knell because of what he did to me yesterday,' then we could say, 'Yes. Pay us five pence, and we'll arrange for him to fall down a manhole.' Would that work?"

"If it did," said Frank, "it would be worth more than five pence."

"Let's try," said Jess.

So they spent the rest of the evening making a notice. When it was finished, it read:

OWN BACK LTD.

REVENGE ARRANGED

PRICE ACCORDING TO TASK

ALL DIFFICULT TASKS UNDERTAKEN

TREASURE HUNTED, ETC.

The last two lines were put in by Frank, because he said that if they were going to arrange things like booby traps for Buster Knell, then they might as well agree to *any* dangerous task. Jess put in the Ltd. to make it look official.

"Though it shouldn't be, really," she said, "because we're not a proper company."

"Yes," said Frank, "but if anyone asks us something too difficult, we can always say it means Limited Own Back, and we don't touch things too big for us."

The next morning, they pinned the notice to the back of the potting shed, where it could be seen by anyone who went along the path beside the allotments, and sat in the shed with the back window open to wait for orders.

All that happened, that entire day, was that two ladies exercising their dogs saw it and shrieked with laughter.

"Oh, look, Edith! How sweet!"

"Limited, too! The idea!"

Frank and Jess could hear them laughing about it all down the path.

"Take no notice," said Jess. "Just think of when the shekels start to pour in."

That was all very well, but Frank began to wonder if they were going to spend the entire Easter holiday sitting in the potting shed being laughed at. It was a dismal place at the best of times, and the view over the allotments always depressed him. They were dank and low. Beyond them, there was the marshy, tangled waste strip beside the river where everyone threw rubbish, and under the trees, the hut thing where old Biddy Iremonger lived. The only real house in sight was as damp looking and dreary as the rest—a big square place, the color of old cheese. The trees had been slow to put out leaves that year, so it was all as blank and bleak as winter.

The next day was, if anything, worse still. To start with, it was raining on and off, with a cold wind steadily blowing showers up and away again. Drafts whined through the potting shed and fluttered all the cobwebs. Jess and Frank sat in their coats and began to think their idea was a failure.

"And we can't even buy sweets to console ourselves with," Jess was saying when somebody rapped on the window.

They looked up to see old Mr. Carter, who had the nearest allotment, leaning on the sill of the potting shed window.

"This your notice?" he asked.

"Yes," said Frank, feeling foolish and rather defiant about it. "Why?"

Mr. Carter bent down and read the notice, out loud, so that Frank felt even more foolish by the time he finished, and Jess went very pink. "My, my!" said Mr. Carter. "Just wait till the prime minister hears of this. He'll have you in his cabinet. Got any customers yet?"

"Not yet," Frank admitted.

"We've not been in business long," Jess said.

"Well," said Mr. Carter, "I can't help with the revenge part, but I know where you'll find some treasure."

"Do you? Where?" they said. Jess reached for her notebook to take down the details.

"Yes," said Mr. Carter. "Rainbow, this morning. Ended right beside Biddy Iremonger's place. Saw it with my own eyes. You dig there, and there'll be a crock of gold for you." And before either of them could answer, he went away laughing.

"*Beast!*" said Jess.

Frank was too angry even to say what he thought. Instead he suggested taking the notice down. Jess said that would be giving in too easily.

"Let's keep it the rest of today and tomorrow," she said. "Maybe the news will get round."

"Then we'll have the whole town knocking on the window to laugh at us," said Frank, and he went indoors to cadge some biscuits to cheer them up with.

They were eating the biscuits when they heard quite a crowd of people coming along the path. There was a noise of wheels turning and sticks being trailed along the allotment railings and the fences of the gardens. There were also loud, crude voices, swearing. Frank wished most heartily that Jess had agreed to take the notice down. He did not even need to hear the voices to know that it was Buster Knell and his gang—and, to judge from the language, Buster Knell and his gang in a very bad mood indeed. They all stopped outside the potting shed, and Jess said afterward that she saw the air turn blue.

"Cor! Take a slimeballing look at this!" said someone. "Look, Buster."

"Degutted Own Back!" said someone else.

Frank and Jess sat and looked at each other, while yet another boy read the notice out in a jeering squeaky voice. "Whose slimy idea is this?" he said.

"Eyeballs-in-salsa Pirie kids," they heard Buster say. They knew it was Buster, because his voice was louder and his language nastier than any of the others. "Always got some puke-crusted idea or other."

"Fwank and Jessie," squeaked someone. "Come on, let's tear it down."

The whole gang agreed, at the tops of their voices and the full width of their language. Frank and Jess had resigned themselves to losing their notice when Buster shouted:

"No! I got a much better degutted brains-in-gravy

idea than that. Wait a slimeballing minute, can't you!" Then, before Frank and Jess had time to escape from the shed, he was pounding on the window, yelling, "Anyone in? You too degutted scared to answer? Open disemboweled up, can't you!"

There was nothing else for it. Frank got up and opened the window. Buster put his arms on the sill and pushed his face inside. It was not a nice face at the best of times—all thick and narrow-eyed. At that moment, it was mud down one side, and thicker than usual down the other. There was even blood, just a little, on Buster's stumpy chin.

"What do you want?" asked Frank.

"My zombie-burger Own Back," said Buster. "Like it says. And you slimy-puke owe me ten pence, anyway."

"So?" said Frank, as bravely as he could. Beyond Buster was all the gang, glowering and muddy, carrying sticks and air guns, and towing their usual number of homemade go-carts. They never moved without all this equipment if they could help it, and they knew how to use it, too.

Buster stuck his face sneeringly into Frank's. Jess began gently collecting flowerpots for ammunition. It looked as if they were going to need all they could get.

"I'll let you off that disemboweled ten pence," said Buster, "if you can get me my oozing Own Back on that

8

slimy stomach-maggot scum. Only I bet you're too oozing scared."

"No, I'm not," said Frank. "Who do you mean?"

"Disemboweled scum," said Buster. "Vernon Wilkins. Just look what he done to me. Here, take a look." He pushed his hand toward Frank's face and held it open, palm upward. On it was something small, dirty, and red at one end. "See that?" said Buster. "That's a tooth, that is. That curried-tonsil scum knocked it out for me. What do you say to that?"

The only thing Frank could think of to say was that it was rather clever of Vernon Wilkins, but he did not dare say that.

Buster pushed his hand farther into the shed. "And you," he said to Jess. "You take a degutted look, too. A good long, stomach-juicing look."

So Jess was forced to come and inspect the tooth, too. She brought a flowerpot with her, just in case. It was a double tooth, worn down to a flat disk shape. "Yes," she said. "What do you want us to do about it?"

"Get one of his," said Buster. "You're arranging disemboweled revenge, aren't you? Well, you go and knock me out one of Wilkins's pineapple-puking teeth and bring it back here so I can see you done it. Then I'll let you off that ten pence."

"It's worth more than ten pence," said Jess.

"Is it?" said Buster. "What's the zombie-toenail matter? Do you want to lose a tooth, too?"

"Shut up," said Frank. "When do you want it?"

"It'll take at *least* an hour," said Jess.

"All right," said Buster. "Meet you back here in an hour. And you'd better bring that slimy poisoned-unwinding-bowel tooth with you, or it won't be only ten pence you owe me." Then he took his hand, and his tooth, and finally his face, away from the window and led his gang clattering and wheeling and swearing away up the path.

Jess and Frank stared at each other and felt that everything had gone wrong. The idea seemed to have turned back to front. Instead of other people asking them to get their Own Back on Buster Knell, here was Buster Knell sending them for other people's teeth. The nasty thought was that Vernon Wilkins was a good two years older than Frank and if he could actually knock a tooth out of Buster's head, then there was no knowing what he could do to Frank.

"And it was only a baby tooth, too," said Jess. "I bet it was ready to come out, anyway. What shall we do, Frank?"

"Go and see Vernon, I suppose," said Frank.

So Jess wrote out another notice, which read:

and this they propped in the window of the potting shed, before getting out their bicycles and pedaling off to find Vernon.

Vernon lived just outside the town, because his mother and father worked for the people in the big house on the London Road. Luckily, this was the same side as the allotments and the Piries' house, but it was still some way. It came on to rain again while Frank and Jess were cycling there.

"All for nothing, too," Frank said miserably, bending his head to keep the rain off his face. "If we get a tooth, it'll only be for ten pence I owed him, anyway. Oh, I hate Buster Knell."

"It's quite horrid," Jess agreed. "Just like the Bible. You know—an eye for an eye, a tooth for a tooth—or whatever it is."

"Is that Bible?" said Frank. "I thought it was: If thine eye offend thee, pluck it out. Buster's eye offends me. Both his eyes. And I bet mine are going to offend Vernon."

"If his eye offends thee, black it," said Jess. "Only Vernon's West Indian, so it won't show."

The shower blew over. By the time they reached the

London Road, the sun was shining brightly and bleakly. Frank and Jess propped their bicycles outside the tall iron gates of the big house and walked rather slowly inside the grounds. It could not have been more awkward. The Lodge, where Vernon lived, was just round the corner from the gates. Vernon was sitting on the doorstep. As Frank and Jess came up, they heard his mother saying something inside the Lodge, so they knew that whatever they did or said to Vernon his mother would hear. To make things even more awkward, Vernon was minding his tiny sisters, who were all three playing happily round him in the mud, and the youngest, as soon as she saw Jess, came toddling up, smiling in the most friendly way imaginable. It could not have been less like a tooth-hunting expedition.

Vernon looked up and saw them. "What do you want?" he said, not unpleasantly, but a little guardedly.

Jess just could not think what to say. She did not know Vernon at all well, but his littlest sister had plainly decided Jess was a great friend. She took Jess's hand and beamed up at her.

"Er," said Frank. "One of your teeth, I'm afraid."

"I got none loose," said Vernon. "The last one came out a year ago. You have to go without."

"You don't happen to have kept one, do you?" Frank asked, rather desperately.

"No," said Vernon. "What for?"

Frank looked at Jess for help. Jess held the little sister's hand tightly, for encouragement, and said, "Buster Knell wants it, Vernon. He says you knocked one of his out just now."

Vernon's face became what Jess thought they meant when they said "a study." Anyhow, she could tell he was surprised, pleased, indignant, and suspicious, all at once. "So I did," he said. "What's it got to do with you? You in his gang now?" Then he stood up.

"No," said Frank fervently. Jess backed away, towing the little sister with her. Vernon was quite frighteningly tall.

"Then why do you want a tooth off me?" asked Vernon.

It was a natural enough question. Frank felt very stupid having to answer it. He tried to explain about Own Back Ltd., and the more he explained, the more stupid the whole idea seemed. Vernon did not help at all. At first he was puzzled; then, as he saw the idea, he seemed more and more amused. Then, when Frank had finished, Vernon suddenly stopped grinning and said, "It was evens, anyway.

He'd no call to send you for teeth. His lot set on me with sticks while I was doing the papers, and I got this. Look."

Vernon held out his arm, and Frank and Jess were once more forced to make an inspection, this time of a very nasty-looking scratch all down the inside of Vernon's arm.

"Have you put something on it?" Jess asked. "I wouldn't put it past them to tip their weapons with poison. Then it's not fair, Frank, wanting a tooth, too, is it?"

"I suppose not," Frank agreed, wondering what Buster would do to them with his sticks. "How did you knock his tooth out, Vernon?"

"Didn't know I had," Vernon said cheerfully. "I just knock him down and get out. Nice to think he lost a tooth through it."

"Except it was only a baby tooth," said Jess. "Which makes it unfairer than ever."

"Was it?" said Vernon. "Sure? Then I think I got an idea to settle it. Wait a moment." He darted away round the side of the Lodge, and came back a second later dragging his younger brother by one arm. "Silas got one all ready to go," he said. "Open up, Silas."

Silas squirmed and protested. Jess felt rather sorry for him. It seemed very hard luck on Silas, particularly as Vernon never thought to ask him if he minded. He simply tipped back his brother's head, wrenched his mouth open, and plucked the tooth out as easily as the eye in the Bible. Silas roared. Frank felt rather glad it had not happened to be an eye that Buster had sent them for. Silas, when he saw the tooth being passed over to Frank, roared louder than ever.

"Vernon," called Vernon's mother, "what you do to Silas?"

"Nothing," called Vernon. "Pulled that tooth out for him."

"But, Vernon," Jess said, "it's *his* tooth, and if you give it to us, that means he won't get any money for it."

"I'll give him five pence," Vernon said hastily. It sounded as if Silas's roaring was going to bring Mrs. Wilkins out any second. Vernon fetched out a coin and pushed it into his brother's hand. "There. Stop," he said.

Silas stopped, in midroar, with a set of tears halfway down his cheeks, and closed his fist round the five pence. He looked at Frank and at Vernon so resentfully that Frank felt he ought to explain a little.

"We need your tooth," he said. "It's terribly important. Really. We've got to give it to Buster Knell, because he told us to bring him one of Wilkins's teeth."

Silas looked more resentful than ever, but Vernon laughed. "So then you don't need to say which Wilkins," he said. "That'll settle it."

15

"But it's still not *fair*," said Jess. "Because you've lost five pence."

Frank wished Jess would not always find something to argue about, particularly things which were quite true. He remembered Mr. Prodger said Vernon needed money. "I tell you what," he said to Vernon, "when we've earned some money out of Own Back, we'll pay you back. Okay?"

"Fine," said Vernon. "Maybe I'll send you a customer."

"That'll be lovely," said Jess. She disentangled herself from the little sister, who showed an inclination to roar like Silas. Vernon had to pick her up. Then the Piries mounted their bicycles and pedaled home with the tooth, rather perplexed to find that, far from earning any money, they were now five pence in debt again.

"Well," said Frank, trying to look on the bright side, "we've got it down by half. Maybe we'll get it down to two pence with the next customer."

"Only if whoever it is pays us real three pence," said Jess.

Nevertheless, when, a quarter of an hour later, the gang began to muster in the path by the allotments, grinning, flourishing sticks, and plainly ready to give those disemboweled Piries lawfully what-for, Frank felt it was worth five pence. They waited until Buster himself hammered on the window. Then Jess shoved it open in his face and held out the tooth in a silver-paper tart dish.

"There you are," she said triumphantly. "Wilkins's tooth, just as you said."

Buster glowered at it, then at Jess and Frank. "I bet it's slime-puking not. It's one of yours."

"It is not, then," said Jess. "Look." And she bared her teeth at him. "See. No gaps."

"Then it's one you kept. Or one of his," said Buster.

Frank came up and bared his teeth, too. Luckily, he had no gaps, and only one tooth loose, at the back.

"And we always burn ours," said Jess. Then, because a horrid thought struck her, she left Frank to do the talking.

Buster looked incredulously from the tooth to Frank, and back again. "This is Wilkins's tooth?" he said. "Honor bright and may you die?"

"Honor bright and may I die," said Frank. "If you want it, take it. And don't forget I don't owe you ten pence now."

"No. All right. I let you off," said Buster. He was too astonished, and too respectful, even to swear. He took the tooth. Frank slammed the window on him, and on all the gang crowding round to inspect the tooth and exclaim as if they had never seen one before.

"That's that!" said Frank thankfully.

"Oh, I do hope so," said Jess, "because I've just realized Vernon hasn't any gaps either, and—and—"

"That's his lookout," said Frank. "If he's got any sense, he'll paint one out or something."

17

Jess had not the heart to speak of her really horrid idea just then. Instead, she watched the gang moving unusually quietly away along the allotments, and tried to think on the bright side. "There is one thing, Frank. If they think you can knock out Vernon's tooth, they won't bother you again."

Unfortunately, she was completely wrong.

Two

After the affair of Wilkins's tooth, both Frank and Jess had secretly had enough of Own Back, but since they owed Vernon five pence, there was nothing for it but to stay in business for another day at least. So they sat in the shed for the third day and, all the while, Jess worried about Silas Wilkins's tooth. She had lain awake at night worrying. Now, that morning, she just had to tell Frank her horrid idea.

"Frank, I wish we hadn't *given* them the tooth. I keep thinking of witch doctors. You know, when they want to hurt a person, they take a tooth or just a hair from the person, and do awful things to it. Suppose Buster does? And then it'll be poor little Silas who suffers, not Vernon at all."

"But it's not real," Frank said uneasily. "They always tell you witch doctors can't *really* do magic—only that people *think* they can. Anyway, you know what that gang's like. They're bound to lose it before they decide what to do with it. Or they'll get them mixed up and magic Buster's."

"Oh," said Jess. "I do hope they *do*. And give Buster face-ache for weeks."

"Months," said Frank, who had suffered a great deal more from Buster than Jess had. He was thinking of saying that Own Back could offer to do the magicking, and get the teeth mixed on purpose, when Jess noticed that someone was tapping on the window.

She jumped up to open it. Frank followed her, and found two pale little girls outside, hand in hand, their hair flapping in the wind, looking up anxiously at the window. He knew them a little by sight. They were the funny, old-fashioned girls who lived at the one house you could see from the potting shed—the cheese-colored one. He knew the elder one was called Frances Adams, because people shouted "Sweet Fanny Adams!" after them sometimes, because they were so odd and because the younger one walked with a limp.

"Do you mean this notice?" asked the elder one.

"Yes," said Jess. "Of course. You don't think we put it up for fun, do you?" She was being rather haughty with them, partly because they were so peculiar, and partly because she was afraid they were going to make fun of Own Back like everyone else.

But the two little girls were in deadly earnest. The elder said: "And when you say difficult tasks, you mean that, too?"

"Yes," said Frank. "But the price goes up if it's really difficult."

They nodded. "This is," said the elder, and Frank felt rather mean. They did not look as if they had much money. They wore funny patched aprons, like Victorian children, and their faces were thin and hungry. Their two pairs of big eyes stared at Frank and Jess like a picture of famine.

"What do you want us to do?" said Frank.

"Get us our Own Back," said the elder.

"On Biddy Iremonger. She's a witch," said the younger.

"I don't think she *is*," said Jess. "Mummy says she's just a poor old creature, and a bit wrong in the head."

"Yes, she *is*," said the elder. "She put the evil eye on Jenny last summer, and Jenny's foot's been all wrong ever since."

"The doctor says it's nothing," said Jenny, "but I can't walk and she did it."

"And," said Frances, "if you can do her down, we've got a gold sovereign that belongs to us and we'll give it you. Promise."

Frank and Jess were both dismayed. The little girls stared so intensely—and the idea of a whole gold sovereign was overpowering. The worst part was how much they seemed to mean what they said.

Frank asked feebly, "What do you want done to her?"

"Anything," said Frances.

"Everything," said Jenny.

"Suppose," said Jess, trying to be businesslike, "we get her and make her take it off Jenny. Would that do?"

They nodded fervently. "But if she won't," said Frances, "do something nasty to her instead. Very nasty."

"All right," said Frank. "If you want."

"Thank you," they both said and, before Jess could think to make further arrangements, they hurried away down the path. Frances pulled Jenny, and Jenny did indeed limp badly.

"Oh, dear!" said Jess, and then, after a moment, "It's probably only rheumatism. Mummy always says how damp that house looks."

"Jess," said Frank, "we can't go and—and *do* things to Biddy Iremonger, can we? Even if she is a witch."

"But she's not," said Jess. "It's just them. Biddy's only funny in the head. And I don't think we can take their sovereign, anyway. It's not money any longer, is it?"

"So what had we better do?" Frank said helplessly. "Go and talk to Biddy? It worked with Vernon."

"I don't know," said Jess. "Maybe if Jenny thinks it's Biddy, then if we can get Biddy to say she's taken it off somehow, Jenny might feel better. Would that work?"

Someone else was reading their notice while Jess talked. Frank happened to look sideways, and saw a horse—or perhaps a pony—outside, with a boy on its back who was bending down to read the notice. "Except it wouldn't be Own Back," Frank said, watching to see if they had another customer. But it seemed they had not. The boy's smart boots moved against the pony, and the pony went on past the window. Jess looked up, hearing the hooves. "Who was that?" Frank asked.

"That's the boy from the big house," said Jess. "Where the Wilkinses work. I wish he'd stayed. Kate Matthews thinks he's super. She's always on about him."

"He thinks he's too super to come near us, then," said Frank. "And that's a pity, because I bet he's got real money. Anyway, Jess, let's try going to see Biddy, shall we?"

"All right. I suppose we'd better."

Jess was just about to put up her AWAY notice, when they heard hooves clumping again and the big shape of

23

the pony filled the window. Jess hurriedly put down her notice and backed away. Both she and Frank held their breath while the boy sat on the pony and did nothing. Then, when Frank was beginning to whisper that they might as well go, the boy reached out his riding crop and rapped it on the window.

"Hark at Lord Muck!" said Frank.

Jess backed right to the potting shed door, pulling Frank with her. "Oh, you go, Frank. I daren't."

"Then let go of me. Coming, my lord, coming!" said Frank.

"Frank! Don't be silly!"

"Who's silly?" said Frank, and tore himself free. He went to the window and opened it. "Yes?" he said, looking up at the boy and wondering what was so super about him. Nothing, Frank thought, but the boy's own idea of himself. He was just a freckled boy with red hair and a haughty look.

"Are you Own Back?" asked the boy.

"Half of it," said Frank. "The Limited half's by the door."

That, of course, made the boy bend down and peer into the shed, and brought Jess up beside Frank, very pink and swinging her hair angrily. "He means me," she said, and gave Frank a sharp kick on the ankle to teach him a lesson.

"Then I'd like you two to do a job for me," said the boy.

"What? Revenge-difficult-feat-or-treasure-anything-to-oblige," Frank gabbled in a way that was meant to be rude. Jess kicked him again.

The boy shifted about, as if he could see Frank did not like him. "Vernon told me about you," he said. "If you must know."

Jess glared at Frank, and Frank realized he had better be polite if they were ever to earn that five pence. "What was it?" he asked. "Some kind of Own Back?"

"Yes," said the boy. "Actually." His freckly face screwed into stormy lumps. "I want you to do something about those beastly Adams kids. I can't stand them. And I don't know what to do about them."

"What?" said Jess. "You mean those two funny girls who live over there?" She pointed to the cheese-colored house.

The boy looked. "I don't know where they live," he said. "If you've got them on your doorstep, I pity you. Frankie and Jenny Adams, they're called, and one limps. And they drive me mad. They're always round our house, calling names and saying it's really their house. As if I could help living there! No matter what I'm doing, one of them bobs up and says it should be hers. And I'm not sup-posed to hit girls, for some reason, so I can't stop them."

"You want us to try to stop them?" asked Jess.

25

"At least go and call *them* names," said the boy. "Show them what it feels like."

Both Frank and Jess rather thought the Adams girls knew what it felt like, but they did not like to say so. Frank said, "Or something to teach them a lesson?" and the boy nodded. "And I think we'd charge ten pence," said Frank, because that seemed reasonable.

The boy shifted again, until his pony stamped irritably. "I was afraid you might," he said. "I'll try and get it, but I'm a bit short, actually. I broke a greenhouse last week, and they stopped my pocket money. Couldn't I give you something else instead? Exchange and barter? I've got a watch or a camera you could have."

The Piries' hearts sank. No money again. Not even a fellow feeling for someone else without pocket money prevented Jess from feeling a little cross with the boy.

"You should really have brought some money," she said severely. "We don't do it for goods. And we've both got watches."

"I'll try," said the boy. "Maybe I'll wangle some money. But I'd got desperate, actually, and when Vernon told me about you, I thought I'd see. Honestly, you don't know what it's like. They're *always* there." He did, to do him justice, look desperate, in a fretful sort of way.

"All right," said Frank. "We'll do it. On condition that you get us some money if you possibly can."

"I'll try," said the boy. "Honestly. Shall I come back tomorrow, or do you need longer?"

"No. Tomorrow will do," said Frank.

"Thanks," said the boy, and he seemed genuinely grateful.

They watched him ride away down the path, scattering loose cinders with the pony's feet, and they felt more than ever perplexed at the difficulties of Own Back.

"And it ought to have been so *profitable!*" said Jess. "What's wrong?"

"I don't know," said Frank, "but I know this lets us off Biddy Iremonger. We can just go and tell those kids that we won't do it because they shout after Lord Muck. What's his real name?"

"Martin Taylor," said Jess. "No, Frank, that's not *fair*. They asked us first, and she does limp terribly. We'll have to see them about him afterward."

"I can't think," said Frank, "why he doesn't hit them secretly, even if he's not supposed to. I would. And what's she got to go and be called Frankie for? It's so *muddling.*"

"Come on," said Jess. "Let's get it done before lunch. Then I vote we close."

So they put up the AWAY notice once more and let themselves out of the back gate onto the allotment path. There was a strong wind. The sun shone bleak and bright, but not at all warm. Frank shivered. He told himself it was the wind and the old-cabbage smell the wind blew out of the allotments which made him shiver. But it was not. He was dreading Biddy Iremonger. And, to make matters worse, Mr. Carter was digging on his allotment and called out to know if they had found the treasure yet.

"Take no notice," said Jess, and with her nose stuck haughtily in the air, she pushed open the gate to the path that ran beside the allotments to the river.

The path took them down to the tangled, rusty fence on the river side of the allotments. It was the kind of fence nobody cared for. The parts of it that were not old, old barbed wire were made of bits of iron bedsteads, and it was held in place just by being overgrown with whitish wintry grass and brambles. The path dwindled to a muddy rut where the fence met the wall, and squeezed its way up and round a loose piece of old bed. Frank and Jess squeezed with it, into the waste, white grass beside the river.

It was hot there—airless and smelly—because the big willow trees seemed to keep the wind off, and because it was low lying. The river spread out secretly under all the white grass. If you walked off the path, you were in squelching, oily marsh. And it was full of rubbish—some of it buried under the grass, some of it thrown on top. There was a heap of tins beside the fence. A few steps farther on, there was all that was left of an old bicycle sticking out from under the grass. The path went carefully round its front wheel. When Frank had been younger, he had thought this the most exciting place in the whole world. You never knew what you might find—motor tires, mousetraps, buckets, and bedsprings. But he was now too old to find it interesting. It depressed him instead. He particularly hated the muggy, sweetish smell in the place.

"Pooh!" said Jess. She marched on ahead, sending up musty smells from under her feet straight to Frank's nose.

Biddy Iremonger's hut was under a big hollow tree beyond a clump of brambles. It looked as if it might have been a boathouse once. It was wooden and settled slopingly down the riverbank. In front of it was a patch of bare earth, and heaped carefully round that were petrol drums and paint tins, to make a sort of wall. The path, as if it were scared at the sight, took a wide bend away from the hut and hurried, twisting, on to the footbridge over the river just beyond. There was a sort of track leading to the hut, however, and Frank and Jess cautiously took it.

Biddy Iremonger's black cockerel flew up to the roof of the hut when it saw them coming. The four black hens ran for shelter in a petrol drum. As soon as Jess set foot in the bare patch, Biddy's cat leaped up, almost under her feet, and spat. It was a scrawny patchwork cat—ginger, tabby, black, and white, all at once—and it seemed scared of everyone except Biddy. It ran away from Frank and Jess, crouching and cringing, to the doorway of the hut. There it turned and spat again before it ran inside.

Frank and Jess, their nerve rather shaken by the cat, stood side by side in the bare patch, nearly overwhelmed by the hot, musty smell, which seemed worse than ever near the hut. Before they could think of what to do, Biddy Iremonger herself came slowly shambling out of the door of the hut and stood nodding at them cheerfully.

She was wearing at least three dirty sweaters and a skirt from a jumble sale, with sort of sacking trousers showing under the skirt. She had a sack round her shoulders, too, like a shawl. Her hair, as usual, was put into at least six skinny plaits, which were looped up anyhow and held fast by curlers and paperclips. You could not see easily what her face was like—apart from its being very dirty—because she wore such enormously thick glasses. Her feet were in odd plimsolls, and her legs, below the sacking trousers, were bare and purple and swollen, so that her ankles drooped over her plimsolls. Jess was chiefly struck with how cold Biddy must be, living in a hut in all weathers. Frank just wished they could go away.

"Good morning," said Biddy. "It's nice to have some warmer weather, isn't it?" She looked up at the branches of the willow tree, where powdery bright green buds were just beginning to show. "Yes," she said. "We can allow it to be spring before long, don't you agree, my dears?"

Neither Frank nor Jess knew what to reply. The oddest thing about Biddy Iremonger was that she was educated. She had a sharp, learned voice, rather like Jess's school-teacher, which, when she spoke, made it very difficult to imagine her putting the evil eye on people—or, indeed, doing anything that was not just harmless and a little odd. So Jess and Frank nodded, and mumbled things about "nice day" and "no rain," and Jess went on bravely to add, "There's a bit of a wind, though."

"Not down here," said Biddy. "This little nook is beautifully sheltered."

Then they all stood there without talking. The cockerel stalked to the edge of the roof and peered down at the Piries. The cat came slinking to the door and stared up. Biddy just waited, nodding, with a cheerful smile, as if she was sure they had just called to pass the time of day and would be going away any minute now.

Frank and Jess very nearly did go. It seemed such a shame to bother this poor, silly old lady because the Adams girls had got it into their heads that she was a witch. It was only Jess's strong sense of fairness that kept them there. Jess took hold of Frank's sleeve, took a deep breath of the muggy air, and said, "We're sorry to bother you, Miss Iremonger, but we wanted to speak to you about—about Jenny Adams."

"Oh, yes? What about her?" said Biddy, cheerfully and sharply.

"Well," said Jess, feeling very silly, "she—er—she can't walk, you know."

Biddy shook her head at Jess and answered, quite kindly, "Now, my dear, that's not really accurate, is it? She can walk quite well. I've seen her limping about rather nimbly, considering."

Jess felt so foolish that she hung her head down and could not say a word. Frank had to clear his throat and reply. "Yes, we know," he said. "But her foot's bad all the same, and she says you put the evil eye on her." He felt this was such a monstrous thing to say to Biddy that his face and his eyes—even his hands—became all hot and fat as he said it.

And Biddy nodded again. "Yes, my dear. She's quite right. I did. I have it in for that family, you know."

Jess's head came up. Frank went suddenly from hot and fat to cold and thin with horror, that anyone could talk as calmly and cheerfully as Biddy about a thing like that. "Why?" he said.

"How unfair!" said Jess.

"Not at all," said Biddy. "One has one's reasons. I have to get my Own Back, you know."

"But look here," said Frank, "she's only a little kid, and she's had it for a year now. Couldn't you take it off her?"

"Please," Jess added.

Biddy, smiling and shaking her head, began shuffling back into her hut. "I'm sorry, my dears. It's none of your business."

"You're wrong," said Jess. "It is our business—exactly. Please take it off."

Biddy stopped for a moment, in the doorway of her hut. "Then, if it is your business," she said briskly, "I suggest you give me a wide berth, my dears. It would be wisest. Because, I assure you, Jenny Adams is not likely to walk freely until she has her heirloom in her hands. Which, in plain language, is *never*. So I suggest you leave the matter there."

Biddy shut the door of her hut in their faces with a brisk snap, and left Frank and Jess staring at each other.

Three

The first thing they did was to get themselves out of Biddy's bare patch and back to the path again. There, halfway to the footbridge, Jess stopped.

"How awful!" she said. "How terrible! Oh, Frank, Biddy Iremonger must be quite, quite mad after all. She ought to be put in a Home."

Frank did nothing but mumble. His skin was up in goose pimples all over, and he did not trust himself to speak. All he wanted to do was to go away quickly. He hurried on along the path toward the bridge.

Jess followed him, saying, "Of course, she may have

been having us on. Mummy says she's got a strange sense of humor."

Frank again said nothing. It seemed plain enough to him that Biddy had meant what she said, and if Biddy believed herself to be a witch, he could hardly blame the Adams girls for thinking so, too. Mad or not, it did not seem to matter. Perhaps witches *were* mad, anyway. What did matter was what they were going to tell Frankie and Jenny, because it looked as if Own Back had let them down. He was wondering just what they would say when Jess grabbed at his arm.

"Oh, dear! Listen, Frank."

There were voices, distant, but getting nearer, loud and crude, and the sound of wheels and sticks. Buster Knell and his gang were in the field on the other side of the river somewhere. Jess and Frank bundled along to where the bridge began. The river took a bend here, which allowed you to look up along the opposite bank. There they could see the gang coming along the bank toward the bridge in a noisy group, about twenty yards above Biddy's hut. They could hear, not clearly, slimy and disemboweled language.

Frank slid quickly down the bank beside the bridge, where there was a tiny beach of gravel. He was hidden there by a bush and some newly sprouting flags, but he could see Buster and the gang. Jess hesitated, then followed him. They crouched side by side, watching the gang come nearer.

"But it's all right," said Jess. "They'll not dare lay a finger on *you*, Frank, after Wilkins's tooth."

"That's what you think," said Frank. "I'm not taking any chances."

"They'll come over the bridge, though," said Jess. "Hadn't we better go across first? Otherwise, they'll be between us and the Adamses' house, and then we'll have to go back past Biddy's hut and I don't think I can *bear* to."

"Shut up," said Frank. "I bet the Adams kids went past it. If they can, you can."

"Between the devil and the deep blue Buster," said Jess. "Oh, dear!"

To their intense relief, the gang turned aside when they were about ten yards off, and went calling and cursing and splashing down into the river. It seemed they were going to ford it. Maybe it was more manly or more exciting, or both, that way. Jess and Frank waited agonizingly, until the smallest boy, in the last go-cart, had been, with cursing and tremendous difficulty, lugged through the water and onto the bank out of sight. Then they stood up and sprinted over the bridge and out into the field beyond. Halfway to the bare, lonely Adams house, they looked back. The gang appeared not to have noticed them. They

36

were milling about in the bushes and rubbish just above Biddy's hut, and no one was looking their way. Rather nervously, Frank and Jess followed the path over to the peeling door in the side of the cheese-colored house, and knocked.

The door was opened, after a lot of hollow-sounding treading about, by a thin, tall, vague-looking lady in a dangling smock. Jess at first thought the lady was covered with blood. Then she saw it was only paint. There was paint on the lady's hands, too—so much that the lady did not seem to be able to touch the cigarette she had in her mouth. She talked round it, through puffs of smoke, and the cigarette wagged.

"What do you kids want, eh? No jobs going, I'm afraid. Bohemian household and all that."

"Could we see Frankie and Jenny, please?" asked Jess.

"Oh, yes. Sure. This way." The lady left the door open and simply walked away inside the house. Frank and Jess, a little doubtfully, stepped inside and followed her down a cold stone passage smelling of mildew and lamp oil. They could not tell which smell was the strongest. Jess thought mildew and did not wonder that Jenny had rheumatism. Frank thought lamp oil. There seemed to be no electricity in the house.

The lady pushed open a door. "Frankie. Friends for you," she said. Then, with her cigarette still untouched and wagging, she went off into another room. Before the door to it shut, Frank glimpsed an easel, with a painting on it.

The two little girls were in a small room that smelled, distinctly, more of mildew than of oil. There were toys about, so it must have been a playroom. But it was, Jess thought, almost as cheerless as the potting shed, and certainly as dark. The reason for the darkness was that outside the window stood a great wooden mill wheel, so old that grass grew on it in clumps, and so big that very little light got past it into the room.

Frankie bounded to meet them, looking so excited that Jess felt mean. "What happened? What did you do to her?"

"Nothing yet," Jess said awkwardly.

Frankie just looked at her, with her great big famine eyes. Jenny, who was crouched up on the windowsill, said, "I knew you wouldn't. Nobody dares to." She was not jeering. She just said it as a matter of fact, rather sadly. She made Frank feel terrible—even worse than Jess was feeling.

"This is—this is a sort of progress report," he said. "We saw her, and she said she wouldn't take it off you. That's as far as we've got."

Frankie leaned forward, with her eyes bigger than ever. "Then go on and do something awful to her. Now you know."

"At least you didn't let her deceive you," said Jenny. "Lots of people won't believe she's a witch, but that's just because she looks jolly and they think she's joking."

"But she isn't joking," said Frankie. "She's wicked. Really."

Somehow, now they had talked to Biddy, Jess and Frank found this easier to believe. Jess still knew, somewhere in the back of her head, that Biddy must simply be mad, but she did not know it strongly enough to say so. All she said was "Yes, I know. She said she's got it in for your family."

Both little girls nodded. "Yes, she has," Frankie said. "So now do something."

"All right," said Frank, "but"—he hesitated, and then said, in a rush, in a rather official-sounding voice, because he felt so mean—"but we've got to do it on conditions, because we can't take your sovereign."

The little girls stared. "Why not?" said Jenny. "It's worth much more than a pound."

Jess saw the point. She shook her head firmly. "It's not legal tender," she said. She was not quite sure what that meant, but she was sure it was the right phrase, and it sounded beautifully official. Frankie and Jenny were impressed by it and stared mournfully at her.

"So we'll do something to Biddy," Frank went on pompously, although he was out in goose pimples again at the mere idea, "if you promise us to stop calling names after—what's his name, Jess?"

"Martin Taylor," said Jess.

"Who?" said Jenny.

"Ginger," said Frank. "Up at the big house. You know."

"Oh, him!" Frankie stuck her head up.

Jenny leaned forward indignantly and nearly overbalanced from the windowsill. "We hate him. He's horrible. He lives in our house. It should be *our* house, but *he* lives there just because we haven't got any money anymore."

"We're going to drive him out," said Frankie.

"Don't be silly," said Jess. "You can't drive him out, because it's his parents, not him, the house belongs to. He can't help living there. It's not fair to go calling him names. He isn't allowed to hit girls."

Jenny grinned. She looked like a wicked elf thing, all curled up on the windowsill. "We know he can't," she said.

"He calls *us* names, too," said Frankie. "And we're not going to stop. So there."

Jess immediately marched away to the damp door. "All

right. Then we're not going to do anything to Biddy. We wouldn't touch her with a barge pole. So there."

There was a painful silence. Jess opened the door and tried to go through it slowly, without looking as if she was waiting. Frank loitered after her. Still neither of the little girls said anything. Frank and Jess had gone most of the length of the stone passage before there was any sound at all. Then, suddenly, behind them, they heard rapid foot-steps—light, heavy, light, heavy. Jenny, down from the windowsill, was following them as hard as she could go.

She ran up to Jess, seized her hand, and smiled up at her. When she smiled, Jess thought, Jenny looked almost as sweet as Vernon's littlest sister. "Please," Jenny said. "Please, Jessica Pirie, do something to Biddy and I'll promise anything." Then her face became all stiff and famine seeming. "Make her die, so that my foot can be better again." Great huge tears came streaming down her cheeks.

Frankie came up without a word, put her arm round Jenny, and led her back to the playroom again. Jess and Frank followed, feeling mean and big.

Jess said, "I don't think it would work, making her die. She'd not be able to take it off then. She said—" Jess looked at Frank. It had been nasty, the way Biddy had said *never*.

Frank shivered. "Jenny," he asked. "What's your heirloom? Or don't you know?"

Frankie answered, because Jenny had her odd apron to her face and was giving out shuddering sniffs into it. "It's an emerald necklace," she said. "Mine's diamonds. Only it went. All the things went."

"Went where?" said Jess.

Jenny shook her covered face. "Don't know. They went. Mother went, too." She gave a big muffled yell, and the whole of her shook.

Frank fidgeted. Everything about these little girls seemed odder every second. He felt he could hardly bear another minute in that gloomy room with the big wheel blocking the window. "Well, the best thing would be to get it back," he said, "but if you can't, we'll have to think of something else to do to her."

"Make her break her leg," said Frankie.

"Or something," Jess said, as cheerfully as she could. "We'll do something, provided you stop calling after Martin Taylor."

"All right," Frankie agreed. "We'll stop, then. It's worth it, isn't it, Jenny?"

Jenny, with her face still covered, nodded violently.

Jess and Frank escaped from the damp house and went home by the road, in the hurling wind. They were so relieved to be outside again that Jess sang and whirled her arms as they went.

"At least we've fixed Martin," she said.

"For no money," Frank said. "Isn't that paint lady their mother, then?"

"No. She's their aunt," said Jess. "But Daddy knows Mr. Adams. He's a bit strange, too. Frank, let's put Biddy off and stay closed for today. I've had enough of Own Back for now."

"I've had so much enough," said Frank, "that I wouldn't mind closing down for good."

"We'll do that," said Jess. "We'll just polish off this bit of business, and then we'll close down."

Four

The next morning, Frank and Jess were in the potting shed discussing what to do about Biddy. While they talked, Jess carefully wrote out a very elaborate curly notice, which was to read CLOSED FOR GOOD. She had so far only got to FOR, and neither of them could think what to do to Biddy.

"An eye for an eye," said Frank. "What about a foot for a foot? Suppose I went and stamped on her toe?"

"She might turn you purple," said Jess. "She might even *be* a witch. What did they use to do to witches in the olden days?"

"Duck them in a pond," said Frank. "Could we push her in the river?"

"Flop," said Jess. "Squelch. She'd lose her glasses. And she'd be *mad*, Frank."

"I thought you said she was, anyway," Frank was saying, when there was a hurried dull thumping on the path outside and the window of the shed was darkened.

"Martin Taylor!" Jess sprang up eagerly and hastened to the window. "At least we can tell him *he's* all right," she said as she pushed it open.

But Martin, it seemed, had not come for his Own Back. He leaned down from his pony to look in the window, and they could tell by his face that something or other was wrong. "Can you two come to the Lodge?" he said. "Vernon's waiting there. He'll explain. But we thought you ought to see Silas."

"See *Silas*!" said Jess. "Whatever for?"

"Oh, I can't explain," Martin said. "Just come and see." And before they could ask him more, he was gone again, with a further swift thumping and a scatter of cinders.

Frank and Jess looked at each other, mystified, but rather appalled, too. If they had known Martin better, they might have thought he was having them on; but he was nearly a perfect stranger, and the way he had talked was as if he were too upset about whatever it was to tell them about it. So, after a second, Frank muttered that he supposed they had better go and see. Jess simply put up the AWAY notice instead of the CLOSED notice and they went to get their bikes.

When they came within sight of the big iron gates, Martin was standing outside with Vernon. The way they both stood was dejected and anxious, and the way Vernon dashed up and seized Jess's handlebars was almost angry, too.

"What did you do with that tooth?" he said. "Give it to Buster?"

"Yes," said Jess, and Frank added, "And you needn't eat us."

"Then Buster *was* telling the truth," Martin said to Vernon. It was clear they were both too worried to bother to quarrel with the Piries.

"I knew he was," said Vernon. He turned to Frank and Jess. "You come and take a look at Silas," he said. "Buster said to me he give the tooth to Biddy Iremonger to give me face-ache. You come and see." And, as soon as Frank and Jess had leaned their bikes against the gates, he led them to the Lodge. At the door, he jerked his head to Martin. "Go and talk to my mum," he said. "If she sees them, she'll throw them out." The haughty Martin, rather to Frank's surprise, went into the Lodge without a word.

As Vernon beckoned them to follow him also, they could hear Martin saying something quite near, and Mrs. Wilkins answering, rather crossly, "How you think I do it today, Martin, with Silas sick in bed?"

Both Jess and Frank were quite sure they ought to go away at once. But Vernon seized them each by an arm and pulled them through a door and into a darkened room beside the front door where, as Jess said afterward, she felt like thieves in the night. Vernon went across to a window and drew one of the curtains. Frank and Jess, thoroughly alarmed and nervous, found they were in a bedroom with bunk beds round the walls. All the beds were empty except the bottom bunk nearest the window, which had Silas lying in it.

"Now see," Vernon whispered.

All Frank and Jess could see of Silas was his face, but that was quite enough. Jess said afterward she had never seen a face so swollen as Silas's was, not even Frank's when Frank had mumps. The only right thing about it was his big resentful eyes, and these stared accusingly up at the Piries. The rest of his face was tight and shiny and blown out like a balloon—so blown out that it was more purple than black.

"Oh, dear!" said Jess. She had her hands to her own face in sympathy. "Isn't it mumps?"

Vernon shook his head. "He had them when I did last year. The doctor doesn't know what it is. But I know. It was Biddy did it."

Silas said nothing. He stared miserably. Frank did not wonder. Neither he nor Jess could think of anything else to say. They stood there in the middle of the bedroom feeling like trespassers, and Jess, at least, wondered if she did not feel like a murderer also. And all the time Silas simply stared at them with his great black accusing eyes.

Meanwhile, Martin must have made Mrs. Wilkins really angry. Her voice suddenly came nearer, talking and talking, until it was clear she was right outside the bedroom door and likely to come in any minute. Frank and Jess felt more like trespassers than ever.

"Quick," said Vernon. "Come on." He opened the window and scrambled out, into the flower bed beneath. Jess and Frank scrambled after him, faster than they had ever climbed out of a window before. Vernon reached back inside to draw the curtain again, and Silas's big reproachful eyes watched all three of them as he did it.

They hurried out to the road beyond the iron gates. While they waited for Martin to finish being scolded and come and join them, Vernon said, "You got to get that tooth back."

There seemed no doubt that he was right. "All right," said Frank. "But how can we get it?"

48

"Go down to her hut," said Vernon. "They said she was a witch, but I never believed it till now. What do you think she'll take to give it back?"

"I don't know," said Frank.

Jess said, "Vernon, you wait here with Frank, and I'll go home and collect all our valuables. I think that's fair, Frank, because we did let Buster get his hands on that tooth."

Frank mournfully agreed. He owned a tiepin which he did not much mind losing, but he had a feeling it would take his watch as well, which he did mind losing. But it could not be helped. He could not condemn poor Silas to spend the rest of his life with his face that shape—particularly as it looked as if it must hurt rather a lot, too. So, while Jess cycled off to collect what she could which might be valuable, Frank sat on the roadside with Vernon and asked him if he had a plan of action.

"I thought," Vernon said, not exactly hopefully, "I take Jess and go and ask Biddy for the tooth back, and keep her talking supposing she says no. Then you and Martin find some way into her hut round the back and look for the tooth."

Frank quaked. But he saw Vernon was right. Obviously Vernon should ask for the tooth, since it was supposed to be his, and Jess had to be there to represent Own Back. Which left Martin and himself to do the dirty work. And Martin did not strike him as the most encouraging companion.

"You listen, you see," Vernon explained, "and if she says no, then you try to get in."

"And suppose," said Frank, "we can't find it."

"Try again, when she's out," said Vernon. "But we ought to ask first. Make it legal."

"And if we get it?" said Frank hopelessly. "Can you take a spell off?"

"I can try," said Vernon. "There's ways. My mum's heard some, and there's books in the library that maybe tell us. Or if we just get it back, that could be enough to do it."

"Or I suppose Biddy might even tell you, if we give her enough," Frank suggested. "It can't matter very much to her, surely, once she knows it's the wrong person with a bad face."

"Depends how much Buster give her," Vernon said, "to make it worth her while. We reckon the gang must have clubbed together for it. They never have much money."

"No," said Frank. "They spend it straight off, if they do have any. We ought to be able to get enough together to buy her off."

When Jess pedaled back, she had their two watches, Frank's tiepin and two bracelets, one which she knew was silver—her charm one—and one which she just hoped was valuable. She put them in a heap on the bank. Vernon had fifty pence, which, from the grudging way he added it to the heap, Frank thought he must have been saving for something special. Vernon more or less admitted that he had been when he said, "It's worth it, seeing it was my fault Silas got like that."

"And ours," said Jess. "Vernon, I've been thinking about spells. Isn't salt supposed to take them off?"

"I heard that, too," Vernon said.

And that, it seemed, was as much as any of them knew about witchcraft. Frank wished they had all been born in the Middle Ages, when people knew about such things. He had horrid visions of them making Silas worse while they tried to uncharm him. Jess said, most unhelpfully, that she knew how to get rid of warts. Vernon, even less helpfully, said it was not warts, it was chilblains. Both of them knew seven different ways of being unlucky, and Frank knew three more, but none of it seemed to help. Martin, when he at last came out to join them, said he knew nothing about it at all.

"Only the first thing seems to be to get the tooth back," he said, and he took off his watch to add to the heap.

"But that's not fair," said Jess, trying to stop him. "You didn't have anything to do with the wretched tooth."

"Vernon's my best friend," said Martin. "So it *is* fair. He's done all sorts of things for me."

So Jess gave in, and took up the heap in both hands before she crammed it into her pocket. "Surely," she said, "this ought to be enough for one little baby tooth. Weighed in the balance, I mean. Even if it was a *gold* tooth."

"I wish it had been," Vernon said glumly. "Then Buster would have bought them all fish and chips with it instead."

They set off, the Piries wheeling their bicycles beside the other two, until they came to the allotment fence. Everyone was anxious and dejected. Frank almost admitted to being scared as well. He did not like the idea of breaking into Biddy's hut—particularly now she really did seem to be a witch. Still, as he looked at Martin walking in front down the path with Vernon, Frank was more encouraged by him than he had expected. Martin was not as tall as Vernon—probably he was a little younger—but he was promisingly solid looking, and he did not try to boss anyone. It was Vernon who seemed to be the bossy one. At least, somehow, they all kept doing what Vernon said.

They separated before Biddy's hut was in sight. Vernon and Jess went on down the path to the hut. Frank and Martin set off to toil through the white grass, over tin cans and old bicycles, through squashy hidden marsh, to the back of the hut. Stale stinks came up under their feet. Both of them sweated and gasped for air.

"You feel you want to open a window," Martin whispered.

Frank nodded but could not think of a reply. He thought he was going to find it very hard to talk to Martin, until after they had each, with a long stride, got themselves onto the firmer ground under the willows, he remembered one thing he could say.

"We stopped the Adams kids for you," he whispered.

Martin said, "Thanks," and began to sidle along the riverbank to the leaning, rotten-looking back of the hut. "You'll have to wait to be paid, though."

"Can't be helped," said Frank, awkwardly.

Vernon and Jess, meanwhile, went very slowly on toward the bare patch in front of the hut. Jess was so frightened that she found it hard to put one foot before the other, for now they knew Biddy was some kind of witch, and Biddy had warned her and Frank to keep away. Vernon, Jess suspected, was almost as frightened as she was. It showed when he tried to make her go first between the petrol drums, and it showed again when the cockerel flew up to the roof. Both of them ducked and put one arm up. Jess nearly ran away, only Vernon caught her coat and would not let her go.

Biddy did not seem to be there. Jess hoped she was

out—shopping or something. She had often seen Biddy out shopping, with a string bag, all stooped over, peering through her glasses and taking big, irregular, swooping steps. Jess prayed she was doing it now. Vernon fidgeted and seemed to get over being frightened.

"I think she's out," Jess whispered.

"Shall we see?" Vernon asked, with a sideways sort of grin at her. Before Jess could stop him, he picked up a stick and hammered at a petrol drum with it.

A hen squawked. The cat darted out of another drum and ran crouching into the hut. It was so fuggy that the echoes died quickly, as if someone had dropped a blanket over Jess's ears. She and Vernon stood in deep silence until they heard a small shuffling inside the hut. Jess gasped. Vernon's eyes blinked whitely over at her. Then Biddy Iremonger came ambling cheerfully out through the door, still wearing her sack.

"Yes?" she said merrily. "Somebody knocking for me?"

"Me," said Vernon. "Us."

"Ah, good morning," said Biddy. "Vernon Wilkins, isn't it?" She took no notice of Jess at all. "Now what do you want, young man?"

"Please," Vernon answered politely, "I would like to buy back the tooth Buster Knell gave you. How much is it, please?"

Biddy put her glasses straight with a big purple hand and peered at Vernon through them. She chuckled. "I don't see much wrong with your face, young man. I don't believe it was your tooth at all. Whose was it?"

"It belonged to my brother Silas," Vernon admitted, shifting about rather. "And I'd like it back, please."

Biddy chuckled so merrily that her plaits leaped and shook. "Oho!" she said. "So that's it, is it? Now we have it. Wilkins's tooth! Oh, my dear Vernon, what a tangled web we weave, when first we practice to deceive. And what sort of shape is your brother's face in today, may I ask?"

"It's all swollen," said Vernon.

"And it hurts him, you can see," said Jess, who thought Biddy was being maddening. "So could you tell us how much it is, please? And how to take it off him."

Biddy took no notice of her. She said to Vernon, "So now you're sorry, I suppose?"

"Yes. Very," said Vernon. "Can we have the tooth, please?"

"Well, you *may*," said Biddy. "But *can* you? *Can* you? That's the question, Vernon Wilkins, that you have to ask yourself. Can you give me anything as valuable as Buster gave me to charm your brother's tooth for him? What can you give?" She asked the last question very sharply and greedily indeed, and peered first at Vernon, then at Jess.

55

Both of them backed away a step. "Three watches," said Jess.

"And fifty pence," said Vernon.

Biddy shook her head as if she thought this was very funny.

"Two bracelets as well," said Jess.

"And a tiepin," said Vernon. "Looked like gold."

"Oh, it is," said Jess.

Biddy wrapped her sack firmly around her and shook her head again. "No," she said. "I've all the gold I need, thank you."

"Then what did Buster give you?" Vernon asked. Jess could see he was three-quarters scared and the rest maddened, just as she was.

Biddy raised a fat purple finger. "Listen," she said. "Listen. Nine tailors make a man, they say. Now, I have nine times nine—or will have—and, believe me, they shall dance the Nine Men's Morris before they're through. Can you offer me nine again? Or ten?"

"I don't understand," said Vernon.

"I haven't the vaguest idea what you're talking about," said Jess.

"Then that's your bad luck, my dears," said Biddy. "I won't part with the tooth for less. Your brother will just have to get used to his new face."

"How can you be so horrible?" said Jess. "He's only little."

"The size of him doesn't concern me," said Biddy, and she began to go back into her hut.

Vernon and Jess both called out to stop her.

"Beast!" said Jess.

"See," shouted Vernon, "I *had* no teeth of my own. How was I to know you'd do this with it? You give me some idea how I can get it back."

Biddy stopped. "I have," she said. "Only you're too dim-witted to understand. And I'm not going to stand here all morning spelling it out. I've better things to do. Maybe Buster will tell you, if you ask him nicely." She chuckled at the idea.

"Please," Jess said desperately, wondering if Frank could hear and what he was doing. "I'm sure you're really kind and nice, Miss Iremonger, and I'm sure you wouldn't like poor little Silas to suffer when it wasn't his fault."

Biddy looked at her sarcastically. "What gave you that idea, Jessica Pirie? I don't care two pins what happens to the little Wilkins. Why should I?"

"But we do," said Jess and Vernon.

Frank and Martin, meanwhile, were slithering in the damp ground at the back of the hut. It had, plainly, been a boathouse once. That end, just above the river, was a big double door, rather like a garage door, all rotted at the foot. The two halves were held together by a rusty chain, which had been padlocked to a couple of even rustier staples. It was clear that one good wrench would have a staple out and the doors open in next to no time.

Frank looked at Martin, whose face seemed as blank and cool as a statue's. "Do you think she means no?"

Martin nodded. "She's just playing cat and mouse. Making Vernon angry. Go on."

So Frank, who was nearest, put out a careful hand, hooked his finger in a staple, and yanked. And it was suddenly agonizing. Frank could not let go. A pain like a huge electric shock shot up his arm in waves. He all but yelled. Before he knew what he was doing, he was down on his knees, pulling with all his might to get his hand free from the staple. It came away at last, and Frank fell back against the doors with a bang that Biddy must have heard. He listened wretchedly, because he could not have gotten away. His arm hurt too much to move.

To his amazement, no one seemed to have heard. He could hear Biddy, quite clearly, saying, "This for you first, little Miss Pirie. You've been trespassing on my business, haven't you? You and your brother. I'll have you know that Own Back is my concern, not yours, and if I hear any more of your activities, I warn you I shall take a very poor view indeed. I may do something extremely unpleasant. Is that clear?"

Jess answered, in her most argumentative way, "I don't see why you should. You've got some customers out of us, if it comes to that."

Biddy gave a great cackle of laughter. "So I have. So I have, but I mean it."

All this time, Frank was leaning against the rotting door. Martin, with a slightly scornful wrinkle in his nose, said, "What's the matter? Shall I do it?"

"Don't *touch* it!" said Frank.

But Martin already had his hand on the staple. Frank heard him gasp. Frank lurched up, seized Martin's wrist in both hands, and yanked his arm clear. Martin, looking very white, collapsed against the doors, too, till the boards bounced. *"Christmas!"* he said. "Sorry, I didn't—*ow!*—understand. This is no good, is it?"

"Let's get out," said Frank.

"Minute!" said Martin. Frank quite understood, knowing what he had felt like. He waited while Martin leaned against the door, bent over, hugging his arm and breathing like a sawmill. While he waited, Frank heard Vernon shouting at Biddy again and Biddy's sharp voice cutting across Vernon's.

"It's no good dancing up and down, young man. I

don't care what people say or do. You must learn that. The answer is: No Never! Wilkins's face can go the way of Adams's foot, and I don't care. I told you, Jessica, that Jenny will walk when she has her heirloom. You may add that Silas will talk at the same time. Now be off, before I set the dogs on you."

"Dogs?" said Jess. Things were getting out of hand and horrible. Vernon had lost his temper completely and, although Jess did not blame him, she found him as frightening as Biddy.

"I'll give you dogs!" Vernon shouted. He picked up a paint can off the oil drums and threw it at Biddy. Biddy did not move, but the tin somehow missed her. Vernon roared with rage and seized another tin. Before he had a chance to throw it, Biddy fetched a whistle from under her sack and blew it.

"Right. Get him!" said Buster. The gang were suddenly all round them in the bare patch, grinning and waving sticks.

"Help!" Jess shouted. Vernon threw the tin at Buster instead, and missed again. Biddy laughed and settled in the doorway of her hut to watch, while the gang closed in. *"Help!"* Jess yelled.

"Come on," said Martin. "I'm okay now." He and Frank pelted round the hut. By the time they reached the bare patch, Vernon was down, under six yelling boys. Jess was fighting three more, and still calling for help. Martin climbed onto the oil drums and jumped on top of Buster. Frank took the easier way, in through the gap, and charged with his head down at the three round Jess. Before long, he was down, too, and as he rolled and punched, he could hear Biddy laughing.

Jess backed up against the drums, kicked them with her heel as she fought, and went on yelling. The thunder she made nearly deafened her. Perhaps Mr. Carter or someone was in the allotments. Jess hoped he might hear and come. She took Buster's special friend, Stafford, by his hair and shook him. Stafford kicked her.

Then, quite unexpectedly, everything was quiet. Jess propped herself against the drums and found Stafford backing away, looking sheepish. The heap of boys beyond was opening. Someone was peeling people off in layers. Jess saw it was a tall, vague-looking man. When she looked at him, he had Buster in one hand and Martin in the other, but he tossed them away, bent down and fished again in the heap, quite absentmindedly. He came up with Vernon and put him on one side. The two boys next scrambled up for themselves and backed away. Frank surged up to one side of Buster.

"Oh, thank you!" said Jess to the man.

Five

It was plain that Biddy Iremonger was extremely
displeased. She wrapped her sack about her, pushed
her face forward in a peering, snaky way, and shuffled out from her hut toward the man.

"What did *you* have to go and turn up for?" she
demanded.

The man gave her a vague, pleasant look. "I brought
the books you wanted," he said. "They're on the drum
there."

"Then go away," said Biddy.

"In a minute," answered the man. "We'll just settle this

roughhouse first, shall we?" He turned to Buster and his gang, who were standing glowering to one side of him. "Beat it," he said. "Go on. There are at least twice as many of you. You ought to be ashamed of yourselves, you little cowards. If I catch you at it again, I'll teach you something you won't forget easily. Now beat it. And drop those sticks."

Sulkily, the gang cast down its sticks and moved off between the oil drums in a hunched and angry group. They loitered heavily up the path, until they reached the big bramble bush that hid the hut from the allotments. There, defiantly, they stopped. The man took no notice of them. He turned to Vernon.

"And you," he said. "You lot get out, too. I can't have you disturbing Miss Iremonger like this."

Vernon nodded and went out through the gap in the drums. Martin and Frank followed him. Jess, before she went, too, tried to say thank you again. The man stopped her by absentmindedly patting her head.

"Go on, little girl," he said.

Jess, rather indignantly, followed the boys. Because the gang was on the path to the allotments, they had to turn the other way, toward the river and the footbridge. The man waited in the gap in the oil drums until they were nearly at the bridge. Buster glowered, but he could do nothing about it. He just had to watch Vernon, Martin, Frank, and then Jess go out across the bridge and make for the safety of the field beyond. As they crossed the bridge, Jess saw the man turn back into the bare patch to talk to Biddy. As he could still see them, Buster and his gang were helpless. The other four were able to hurry out into the very middle of the field beyond the river, where the wind took them and flapped them about.

There Vernon's nose suddenly burst out bleeding. They had to stop and sit on the grass, while Vernon lay on his back soaking all their handkerchiefs in blood, and sprinkling more blood over a nearby clump of cowslips. They were all glad to sit down. Jess's knees were shaking. Frank was bruised all over, and Martin's lip was cut. Frank and Martin tried to explain why they had been unable to get into the hut.

"But it wasn't electrified," Martin kept saying. "There were no wires."

"Should have thought of it," said Vernon through Jess's handkerchief. "Seeing she's a witch. Did you see that paint can miss her? And it was dead for her. I got good aim."

"And miss Buster," said Jess, "at point-blank range, too. They must have come creeping up awfully quietly. I'd no idea they were even near."

Frank looked at Martin, because he had an idea there

was more to it than that. Martin shrugged his shoulders, as if he gave it up. "But did you hear us?" Frank asked. "We both crashed against the hut like elephants."

"No," said Jess. "Not a thing. I couldn't think what you were doing." After that, they all sat very quietly, gloomily pulling up grass, shivering a little in the strong wind, until Jess looked up and said, "But what shall we do about Silas? This has been an awful failure, and I can't *bear* to think of his poor face all tight and shiny like that!"

"Hurts him, too," said Vernon, from under Frank's handkerchief. "What was she on about tailors for? Would that do any good to understand?"

"Haven't the foggiest," said Martin. "Except I know the saying. Elizabeth the First once made a joke about it. It's 'Nine tailors make a man.' I get ragged about it at school—that's how I know, actually." He gave Frank a look which was half ashamed, half daring him to joke about it.

Frank did not feel like joking. "But, if that's right, then she meant Buster gave her *nine men* to do the tooth! He can't have done!"

"How many in the gang?" Jess said, struck by an awful thought.

"Never counted," said Vernon, reaching for Martin's handkerchief.

"More than nine," said Frank. "There always seems hundreds."

Jess was running over people who had been by the hut. She did not know all the names. She had to do it by saying to herself, "Buster, Stafford, Squeaky Voice, Little Eyes, the one with torn trousers, the little glarey one, the one who imitates Buster, the one with black hair, the very fair one— Do you know, Frank, I think there *were* nine this morning."

"Accident," said Frank uncomfortably. "Not even Buster would do that."

"If he did," said Vernon, sitting up cautiously, with all the handkerchiefs held ready, "then we can't equal it. There's only four of us, and I'm not using Silas again."

"Kate Matthews might," said Jess. "As a special favor."

"Still only five," Martin said. "And Kate wouldn't. She's the silliest girl I've ever met, and I know she'd be scared."

Jess was about to defend Kate when Frank said, "So am I scared. We all should be. Haven't you heard what happens to people who sell themselves to evil?"

Jess nodded. "They flourish for a while, but on their deathbeds, evil comes knocking for them and carries them away despite their shrieks. Oh, Frank! Not even Buster would be so stupid!"

"Why not?" asked Martin. "We were considering it."

This made them all quiet again. Jess had a feeling that Frank had managed to pull them away from the edge of a steepling—or was it yawning?—abyss. She gave him a grateful look, but Frank just looked worried.

"So what do we do?" Vernon said at last.

"Jenny's heirloom!" said Jess.

"What about it?" said Frank.

Jess knelt up and tried to explain. "She said Jenny will limp until she finds it. Then she got mad with me and Vernon, and added Silas to it. So neither of them will get better till it's found. Which means we'd better find it."

"But she meant never," Frank objected.

"I know. She thought 'never.' But we mustn't let it *be* never. We must do her down by finding it. I vote we go and ask Jenny more about it."

Vernon got up at once, saying, "Let's go now." Martin, however, muttered, "Oh, *no!*" and stayed where he was.

"It's all right," said Frank. "Honestly. They agreed to stop, provided we did something to Biddy. And this is something."

"But they're such little creeps," said Martin, with his face bunched up.

"Martin," said Vernon, "you come along and don't be so silly. No one told *me* not to hit girls."

Martin, to Frank's relief, got up grudgingly and set off with them across the field to the Adams's great bare house. They were beside the cheese-colored wall, when Jess suddenly clapped her hand to her mouth and said, "Oh, good heavens!"

"What?" said Frank.

"It's all right. I got your handkerchief," said Vernon.

"No!" said Jess. "Oh, *dear*! I've just remembered who that odd man is who rescued us from Buster. He's their father—Mr. Adams!"

"Christmas!" said Martin. Vernon stared at Jess with his eyes getting bigger and bigger.

"Really," said Jess.

"I get you," said Vernon. "Some tie-up, isn't there? Shall we not ask?"

"I think we'd better," said Frank. "It seems the only way to cure Silas."

Very subdued, they went in a group over to the peeling door, and Frank knocked. After the same amount of hollow thumping about inside as before, the door was opened by the same tall, vague lady, who might have had the same cigarette in her mouth for all Jess could tell. At any rate, it looked the same, and wagged in the same way when the lady spoke.

"Wanting Frankie again?" she said. "I think they're in.

More of you this time, aren't there? Seems a wider palette," said the Aunt, looking from Vernon's black face and blood-spotted sweater to Martin's red hair. "Quite decorative," she said, leaving the door open as before and walking away inside. "Red, black, and two fair ones," they heard her say from down the passage. "And bloodstains to tie it all in."

Vernon and Martin hesitated. "She means go in," Frank whispered. He saw what the Aunt meant about bloodstains. Vernon had bled on Jess's coat, and there was more blood on Frank's leg, which he rather thought was his own, not Vernon's, but he did not at all mind if it were someone else's. He hoped it was Stafford's.

Jess led them inside, after the Aunt. Now that it seemed that Mr. Adams might be a friend of Biddy's, the damp smell struck her as very sinister indeed. She wondered if the Aunt was sinister, too, and when they found her waiting outside the playroom door, Jess was fairly sure that she was. The cigarette wagged as the Aunt looked them over again.

"You know," she said, "you four make a very pretty composition indeed. D' you think your parents would object if I tried to get you on canvas?"

"Oh, very much," said Jess at once. "They'd hate it."

"Don't be daft!" said Frank. "They'd love it."

"Okay," said the Aunt. "Come in here, then." She walked into the room where the easel was and stood waiting for them to follow.

"They've got very strong objections," Jess said desperately. "Religious ones. And—and Vernon belongs to an Eastern religion that doesn't allow him even to be photographed."

"I do *not*," said Vernon, looking rather scandalized. "But," he said to the Aunt, "we would like to speak to Frankie and Jenny, please."

"Give 'em a knock, then," said the Aunt. "Have them in here and talk while I get you down. Makes it more natural, anyway."

They seemed to be absolutely caught. Jess could have shaken the boys, Martin for just standing looking haughty—she was beginning to think that it was when he was shy that he looked haughty, but she could have shaken him all the same—and Vernon and Frank for being stupid and getting them caught. She tried to kick Frank, but he moved out of reach to knock on the playroom door. Jess overbalanced against Vernon and started his nose bleeding again.

The Aunt looked interested. "So that's where it all came from," she said. "Like a key?"

"No, thanks," said Vernon. "It's stopping."

"Don't stop it," said the Aunt. "Let it come. It's a splendid color."

Frankie and Jenny came to the playroom door. When they saw Frank, they looked eager, but as soon as they caught sight of Martin and Vernon, their heads went up and their faces went pale and fierce.

"Why did you bring *them*?" said Jenny.

"They're in league against us," said Frankie.

"No, they're not," said Frank. "Not now, anyway. We're all in league against—against—anyway, we've got to talk to you. Heirlooms. Witch. You know. Your aunt wants to paint us, though."

"Oh," said Frankie. "She does that. She caught the milkman yesterday."

Jess pitied the milkman. The two little girls followed the others into the easel room, which was very cold, but much lighter than the playroom, and there it was all very awkward. Nobody could say anything straight out, because the Aunt was there, sketching fiercely, and mixing blood-red and carrot-red paint; and Frankie and Jenny would not talk to Martin, and not much to Vernon, either. Every time Frank or Jess tried to whisper to the girls, the Aunt asked them to sit still.

"Won't be five minutes," she said, at least twenty times.

Frank became quite desperate. To make matters worse, Jess and Vernon were beginning to find the Aunt painting so interesting that they could not take their eyes off her. They seemed to be forgetting entirely what they had come for. Frank looked at Martin, and Martin made a face back. Neither he nor Frank found anything to interest them, except perhaps the discovery that the Aunt did sometimes touch her cigarette—when it was finished, she popped it in a paint tin and lit another. Apart from this, which was not very interesting, it all seemed rather dull.

Frank had another try. "Heirloom," he said to Jenny. "How was it lost, and when?"

Jenny shook her head. "It just went. When we moved from *his* house." She nodded at Martin, and Martin scowled.

"Splendid!" said the Aunt. "Keep scowling."

"When was that?" Frank asked.

"I don't remember," said Jenny. "I was too little. But it was after Mother went."

"Why do you want to know?" asked Frankie.

This was difficult. "Because," said Frank. "Because—"

"We're joined in," said Vernon unexpectedly. "We find it, do her down, and cure you. She did it to my brother, too, see." The two little girls put their heads up. "You got to listen to me," said Vernon, "because we're on the same side now. Is the stuff up at the big house?"

"Sit still, shadow," said the Aunt. "Just five minutes."

"I don't know," said Frankie. "We were both too small. We think it is."

"Hidden?" asked Frank.

"*She* did it," said Frankie intensely. "She's at the bottom of everything."

"It wasn't sold?" Jess asked, tearing her mind away from the Aunt.

"No. It went," said Jenny. "Like the money and the other things."

"Money always goes," said the Aunt. "That's what it's for. Leave them alone, Jenny. They're jerking about like puppets."

For some time, everyone sat without speaking. Then Martin turned to Frank. "Ask them what she's at the bottom of. Remember the man."

Frank turned to the girls. "Did you hear? Because I'm not a wireless. What's your father got to do with her?"

Frankie and Jenny leaned forward. Frank could see they meant to be fierce but did not like to let the Aunt see. "He doesn't believe," said Jenny.

"But he does lots of things for her," Frankie added. "We think she makes him."

"She's after all of us," said Jenny, nodding at the Aunt, to show she meant her, too.

"But *why?*" Jess demanded.

The Aunt stood back. "*Just* five minutes. Then I'll have finished this daub."

Everyone sat stiff and quiet again. This time, the Aunt meant what she said. After five minutes, she wiped her brush, popped her cigarette into the paint pot, lit another, and said, "There. That's that for the moment. Like to look?"

They crowded awkwardly round the canvas. All Frank could see was a pattern of red and blue triangles, and several black ones. They were all wearing blue somewhere, so he supposed the blue was their clothes and the black must be Vernon somehow. Jess thought it was a little disappointing, and Martin was trying not to yawn—or not to grin; it could have been either. Vernon seemed to think it was fine.

"You like it?" the Aunt said to him, and Vernon nodded. "Needs working up," said the Aunt. "But it's coming on nicely. Come again tomorrow."

One of them sighed. Jess said, "I'm not sure we—"

"Nonsense," said Martin unexpectedly. "Of course we'll come."

"Good," said the Aunt. "Show them out, Frankie, and then we'd better see if there's any food."

"There isn't much," they heard Jenny say as they all trooped to the door.

There Frank rounded on Martin. "Whatever made you say we'd come *back*? Isn't once enough?"

"Stop it. He's dead right," said Vernon, and he turned to Frankie. Frankie backed away inside the house and tried to shut the door in his face, but Martin dodged in and put his foot in the way.

"Leave off," said Frankie, pushing at the door. "I'll call names if you don't."

"No, you won't," said Vernon. "We need to come back to ask you more about it. You know what it looks like?"

Frankie nodded. "Sort of. A necklace of green stones. Like glass, rather."

"See?" Vernon said to Frank. Then he said to Frankie, "We'll look in the big house today. Then we'll have to look here. Can you look, too?"

Frankie turned her big eyes from Vernon to Martin as if she was going to refuse. Jess cut in hurriedly. "It's all right, Frankie. It's to do Biddy down. Honestly. If we find it, then you'll have got your Own Back."

Frankie stopped trying to shut the door and thought about it. "Will she be furious?" she asked. "If you do find it?"

"Hopping mad," said Frank, with a shiver running along his shoulders at the thought.

"Then I'll look for it again," said Frankie.

Martin took his foot cautiously away from the door. "Come and help us," he said, "this afternoon. You know the place at least as well as I do."

Frankie thought again. "We may," she said haughtily, at length. "See you tomorrow, anyway." With that, she firmly shut the door.

The four of them turned away and went, rather drearily, round by the road to the Piries' potting shed. They were all feeling rather cold after sitting so long to be painted, and rather gloomy at failing to rescue the tooth. But Jess was thinking thankfully that, at least, once they had found the heirloom, wherever it was, that would be the end of Own Back for good and all.

She was wrong again. Someone had been while they were away. Whoever it was had left a letter for them, stuck under the window of the potting shed and fluttering in the wind. Frank was only just in time to stop it blowing away entirely.

"Oh, drat!" said Jess. "I forgot to put up the CLOSED FOR GOOD notice."

Six

rank unfolded the letter. It was printed, very heavily and badly, in what appeared to be a foreign language. It said:

Erjant Bizniz cum ta too brij schreet kwik
boat Busta an b ayamunga
Am Desprit

"It must be French," he said.

Vernon looked over his shoulder. "It's not. It's just he can't spell. That's how Silas does it. You read it how it sounds."

Jess and Frank, with difficulty, did so, and gathered that they were to go to 2 Bridge Street on urgent business about—

"What?" said Jess.

"Buster and B. Iremonger," read Martin.

"But," said Jess, "people just aren't called Am Desprit. It's not a name."

Martin burst out laughing. "It's not his name. It's what he *is*. Desperate."

"Daren't put his name," suggested Vernon, "in case Buster gets to know."

"Well," said Jess, "desprit or not, we can't see him now. It's lunchtime."

"And we're going to hunt heirlooms this afternoon," Frank said. "He'll have to wait till this evening."

It was Martin's lunchtime, and Vernon's, too. They had to go.

"Come straight up, after," Vernon called.

Frank and Jess shouted that they would, but after lunch, when it came to the point, Jess insisted that it was only fair to call at Bridge Street first. She did not like the thought of anyone being desprit.

"I bet he is, if he's sold himself to Biddy," Frank said. "Serve him right."

"Oh, Frank," said Jess, as she pedaled beside him,

"suppose the penny's dropped, and he finds himself bound slave for all eternity."

"It'll be more than a penny he'll drop," said Frank. "I want five pence at least out of him."

"But we can't *un*sell him," Jess protested. "Not for five *pounds*."

"Yes, we can," said Frank, "if we get that tooth back. Perhaps we should ask fifty pence, come to think of it."

But Frank was unable to ask for anything, because whoever lived at 2 Bridge Street was not at home. Frank clattered the knocker at the narrow front door of the thin little house, until a lady in curlers stuck her head out of the next-door window and told them the whole family was out. She shut the window again before Jess had a chance to ask which family it was.

Frank and Jess sighed, got on their bicycles again, and pedaled off to the big house. Vernon was waiting for them at the gates.

"How's Silas?" Jess asked him.

"Running a fever now," Vernon answered miserably.

"How mean!" said Jess. "How wicked of Biddy! You must be glad it wasn't you, Vernon."

"I wish it was," Vernon said. Jess could see he was quite wretched about it.

"Look, it's our fault, too," she said. "And we'll find that necklace and spite her."

The problem, they soon realized, was where to start looking. The big house, across a large lawn, sitting up on a hill, was very big indeed. It was the kind of house which is all long, blank windows. Behind it, there were stables, sheds, greenhouses, and gardens. There seemed no end of possible places in which to hide necklaces.

"Is it old at all?" Frank asked Martin, who came sauntering down the lawn to meet them. "I mean, could there be secret panels and things?"

"Not that old," said Martin. "There *is* paneling, but the builders had most of it out when we moved in. I know, because I was watching for hiding places. It was rather exciting, actually—except there wasn't anything. But Vernon's thought about it."

Vernon, who was still very miserable, sighed. "Like this," he said. "If it was Biddy hid the stuff, she'd have to do it quick, not to be noticed. And there's not many places left after the builders went at it. So I think we look in the ways out and in the sheds and gardens first."

"What if she buried it?" Jess asked.

"If she did that," Vernon said, sounding very fierce, "then we'll have to go and see her again. Maybe we can push her into dropping hints, like this morning."

"And push ourselves into Buster's arms," Frank said.

"Risk that," said Vernon. "It's worth it. Let's hunt."

They walked up the lawn, trying to decide who should look where. Frank became rather embarrassed. There seemed to be a lot of people around, peacefully walking about the lawn, or wandering in and out of the various doors of the house. They all stared curiously at the children. Some, who were playing croquet at one corner of the house, leaned on their mallets to watch them.

"Who are they all?" Frank asked Martin.

"They're the guests," said Martin. "You knew this was a convalescent home, didn't you?"

Neither Frank nor Jess had known. They mumbled and tried to pretend they had.

"We have to call them guests," Martin explained, "to humor them. They're nearly all retired loonies really, you see, and we call them guests to show them how much better they are. But you don't have to worry. They're quite harmless and sensible most of the time."

After this explanation, Jess hurriedly suggested that she and Frank should hunt in the gardens. The idea of prying about in mad guests' bedrooms was too much for her.

"Okay," said Martin. "Vernon can take on the back hall and the piece of paneling in the kitchens. I'll do the rest indoors, and join you outside if we don't find anything. Don't take any notice of the guests. They're all bored stiff and gape like fishes if anyone hiccups, but they're quite harmless."

Harmless, Jess decided, was not quite the right word. This was after she had left Frank rooting about in the stables and set off by herself into the gardens at the back of the house. There were a whole lot more guests there. Two fat, red ones were playing tennis. A whole line more sat in deck chairs, with rugs over their knees, all along the back of the house. They were all elderly and, as soon as Jess appeared, all their heads turned, as if someone had threaded them on a string and then pulled it.

Unfortunately, there was a long row of stone urns just in front of these guests. Jess went along, searching in each one, and the row of heads followed her every movement. Jess had found ten empty cigarette packets and an old lollipop, when one old lady could plainly bear no longer not knowing what Jess was looking for.

"Have you lost anything, dear?" she asked.

"No. Thank you. It's not me," Jess said. She scrabbled hurriedly in the last urn, and found a toffee. It stuck to her fingers.

"Put it down, dear," said another old lady. "You don't know where it's been."

"Yes, I do," said Jess. "It's been in here for months, by the look of it, and I'd put it down if it wasn't stuck to me."

"Little girls," said a sharp old gentleman, "should be seen and not heard."

"You spoke to *me*," said Jess. "And I'd be invisible if I could, I promise you, the way you all stare."

"How dreadfully *rude!*" said the first old lady. The others all clucked and nodded their strung-together heads until Jess could not bear it any longer. She fled through a door in a wall nearby, frantically trying to unstick the toffee. She got it off her right hand and it stuck to her left.

"Oh, *bother, bother!*" said Jess, running across more lawn with her head down. The toffee fastened itself to her right hand again.

"Little girl!" called somebody. "Little girl, come here."

Jess looked up from the toffee to find that she was in a small, walled-in garden, with trees against the walls. The person who had called her was another lady guest, sitting in another deck chair beside some daffodils. This lady was not as old as the others and she was holding out a paper handkerchief.

"Here you are," said this lady. "Get it off with this."

Jess went over to her gratefully. "Thank you," she said. "Vernon had a nosebleed into mine this morning."

"Oh, yes," said the lady. "I know Vernon. At the Lodge. Are you a friend of his?"

"I suppose so," said Jess, busily peeling the toffee off

her fingers into the tissue. "Business associate would be more like it, though."

"Really?" said the lady. Jess found the lady looking at her very carefully indeed. She was a pretty lady, with clouds of fair hair and big dark eyes, but she made Jess feel uncomfortable. There was something intense about her. Jess began to back away. She had a feeling that maybe this lady was madder than the other guests and, Jess thought, with Biddy and the Aunt, that would make three mad ladies in one day. Two was plenty.

"I'll have to go now," said Jess.

"In a minute," said the lady, so firmly that Jess stood still. "Now," said the lady, "I have a feeling about you, little girl. You've been meddling with people's worse natures, haven't you?"

"I haven't," said Jess, rather indignantly. "I wouldn't know how to."

"I think you would," the lady answered. "Everyone knows how to do that. We may disguise it from ourselves by calling it a kindness to someone else—as I did—or telling ourselves that it's only fair to do whatever it is, but the fact remains that we've done a bad act disguised as a good one. And I have a feeling that's just what you've done."

"I don't *think* I have," Jess said uncomfortably.

"Are you quite sure?" the lady asked, staring up at Jess with her intense dark eyes. "*Quite* sure? You said something about business just now that didn't sound altogether right to me."

Jess twisted her head sideways to avoid the lady's look. "Well, yes, I am here on business," she admitted, and looked round at the daffodils, the trees, and the walls in search of something else to talk about. "Nice weather," she suggested.

But the lady was not to be distracted. "And are you quite sure your business has nothing to do with evil?" she said. "I have to ask you because I've spent the last five years paying for what I did, and I'd hate you to do the same. *Have* you been meddling with people's worse natures?"

"I—I—" stammered Jess. Then she thought of Own Back. She supposed that was just what it was. "Yes, I think I have," she said. "But I didn't *mean* to. It just happened."

The lady smiled sadly. "That's what we all say," she answered. "Someone says: Do me this favor, and I'll give you six pence, or a pound, or whatever it is. And you see no harm, and you do it. I did someone a favor once, for a half-crown bus fare, and it's taken me all this time to work it off. I hope you didn't let whoever it was *pay* you anything."

"No—I—at least, they haven't yet," Jess said. "Should I cancel it, then?"

"Most certainly," said the lady, "if it's anything at all bad. Just in case."

"All right," said Jess. "I will, then." She was longing to get away. This lady made her more uncomfortable than she had ever felt in her life. "Can I go now?" It was worth having no money just to be able to go.

"In a second," said the lady. "I'm going to give you these first. Have you a chain or something to hang them on, so that you won't lose them? They're very precious." She held out her hand and showed Jess two little oval-shaped things. Jess at first thought they were beads, each with a hook in one of their longer sides. "Eyes," said the lady. Jess saw that they were. Each bead was a little tiny model of an eye, one blue, one brown. "They ward off evil," the lady explained. "The evil eye particularly. I'm strong enough to do without them now. So I'll give them to you, because I think you need them more than I do. What's your name?"

"Jessica," said Jess.

"And so is mine!" said the lady. "That is nice. Now, find a chain."

Jess remembered that she still had her charm bracelet in her pocket. She fetched it out, and the lady helped her hook the little eyes on it. They became quite friendly over it. Jess was almost sorry when the lady said, "Now, run along, dear. You'll be safe now, provided you don't do a bad act disguised as a good one."

"Thanks," said Jess. She looked back at the lady when she reached the door in the wall, but the lady was leaning back in her deck chair and seemed to have forgotten about her. Funny, Jess thought. She's nice, even if she is mad. I wonder who she is.

She forgot about it the next minute, however, because as soon as she came out at the back of the house, the row of heads in the deck chairs turned, following Frankie and Jenny, hurrying and limping past the line of urns. Frankie saw Jess and dragged Jenny over to her.

"We came," said Jenny, "but not to look, because we can't think of anywhere we haven't looked, here."

"Then we'd better look in your house," said Jess. "I'll tell Vernon, shall I?"

"Yes," said Frankie. "But Biddy knows you're looking. I know she does."

"How?" said Jess. "Who told her?"

"We think Daddy did," said Jenny. "He does things for her. We told you. And Aunt heard us while she was painting you, and we heard her talking to Daddy, and Daddy went down to Biddy's hut straight after lunch."

"Oh, no!" said Jess. "But couldn't you stop him? I mean, he seems quite nice. Surely he wouldn't do a thing like that if you explained?"

"We have," said Frankie. "But he's in her power, so it's no good."

"But he's grown up!" said Jess. She just could not credit that Biddy could have power over a real grown-up person.

"I know," said Frankie, "but he does what she wants. Always."

"We'd better tell Vernon," said Jess. "Hurry."

The three of them set off again, round the house, and the row of heads once more turned to watch them. Jess was glad when they were out of sight and gladder still when they ran into Frank and Vernon coming the other way. Vernon was gloomy, because he had found nothing. Frank was cross, because he had tried to search the greenhouses and Mr. Wilkins had very sharply ordered him off. He was crosser still when Jess told him Frankie's news.

"Don't tell me she can magic grown-up men," he said. "It's just nonsense."

"I bet it's not," Vernon said seriously. "That's how it looked this morning."

"Yes, it did," Jess agreed.

"It looked like my big toe, then," said Frank.

"But she *knows*," said Jess. "Look." She pointed behind Frank and Vernon.

Everyone looked, and there were Buster and his gang, trotting toward them up the large front lawn.

"*Now* do you believe it?" said Vernon to Frank.

Nobody else said anything. Frankie seized Jenny's arm, and they all five turned and ran. Behind them, the gang screamed and came racing after. Round the house went Vernon, Frank, Jess, looking over her shoulder, and Frankie, towing Jenny. Round the house, close on their heels, came Buster, Stafford, and the other seven. Round to watch them swung the row of guests' heads.

"We'll get you this time, you vampire-sludge scumbag!" roared Buster.

"Lousy stomach-maggot Piries!" yelled Stafford.

"Sweet sliming Fanny Adams!" screamed the rest.

The row of heads turned as they all streamed past. "My gracious! What language!" Jess heard a lady say. The whole row settled its rugs on its knees and watched with interest. Jess could have shaken them all. None of them so much as asked if they needed help.

"My dad's in the greenhouse," Vernon panted.

"I know," said Frank. He was quite sure Mr. Wilkins would not understand, but he pelted after Vernon toward the far corner of the house. Behind him, Jess saw that

Frankie could not pull Jenny fast enough to keep up. She turned back and seized Jenny's other arm. She and Frankie almost swung Jenny off her feet between them, for the gang had nearly caught up. Frank saw the girls were not there and stopped. Vernon at last realized what was happening and ran round in a circle and back to Frankie, shouting:

"Give her here. I'll carry her."

In the confusion, the gang ran on too far and stopped also, in a line, between them and the greenhouses. Buster laughed.

"Gotcha!" said someone.

"You have not!" said Vernon. He lugged Jenny away from Frankie and Jess, and ran on round the house, carrying poor Jenny anyhow, with her head hanging down, and her feet waving in the air. Jess took Frankie's hand, Frank took Jess's, and together they tore after Vernon—slap bang into the middle of the game of croquet. Guests leaped out of their way. Frank nearly fell over one of the balls, and Jess kicked another clean across the lawn into a clump of bushes.

"I say!" said a guest. "That won't do."

"Help!" said Jess.

"I beg your pardon?" said the guest.

"Oh, bother you, then!" said Jess, and chased on after Vernon. And Vernon, unable to see his own feet because of Jenny, tripped over a croquet hoop, dropped Jenny, and fell on his face.

Buster, who had been hanging back at the edge of the game, probably a little nervous of the guests and their mallets, summoned his courage, gave out his very worst word, and led the gang charging out among the guests.

"I say!" said the guest again. "Look here!"

Frankie, with her head down, looking very determined, raced across to Jenny and dragged her up. Frank ran to help Vernon and tripped over the same hoop himself. Jess was left stranded between a row of startled guests and the charging gang. The guests were obviously useless. It was just as useless to run away. So Jess put her head down and charged at the gang.

"You beastly horrible bullies!" she screamed.

To her amazement, all nine of them stopped dead. Buster, who was the nearest, began to back away, screwing his face up against her. "Hey!" he said. "You body-parts well stop that, Jessica Pirie. What are you *doing*?" Behind him, Stafford fell over another croquet hoop in his hurry to get away. Jess could hardly believe it and could not understand it at all, but she went on toward them.

"Stop it!" shrieked two younger ones.

"I say! This is a bit thick!" said a guest. "What's going on?"

"You boil your head," said Buster, "if you can't stop her."

The guest opened and shut his mouth. Before he could say anything, a French window in the side of the house came crashing open, and out onto the lawn came leaping a rather tubby man with a ginger mustache. After him came Martin.

"You bunch of little hoodlums!" roared this man. He came leaping and bounding down on Buster. "Get out of here, or I'll call the police!" he shouted. Jess realized he must be Mr. Taylor, and she blessed Martin for fetching him.

"Save your breath," said Buster. "We're just going." This was true. The rest of the gang, at the mere sight of Mr. Taylor, went scuttling away across the croquet lawn. Stafford was picking himself up to follow. Buster was poised on one leg, ready to run, but he just could not resist being rude first. He put out his tongue before he ran.

Mr. Taylor gave a roar like a lion's and fetched him a swipe that must have made his head ring. "That's for your impertinence!" he said. "Get out!" Buster staggered, shook his head—not meaning to say no, but because his ears were singing—and ran like a weasel after the rest. Mr. Taylor swung round at Jess. "And you! What do you think you're doing, messing up the croquet like this?"

"We're sorry," said Jess.

"She's a friend of mine," Martin said quickly. "They all are, Dad."

"They were chasing us, Mr. Taylor," Vernon explained, limping up beside Martin.

Mr. Taylor looked them all over, including Frankie and Jenny, pulling his mustache suspiciously. "Oh, they are, are they?" he said. Then he took a dive round at Martin. "Then, if they're your friends, boy, you should know better than to let them create this kind of disturbance. All over the croquet! It's too bad, Martin! Get them away. Take the lot of them inside and give them tea, or something. Only—" Mr. Taylor put his hands in the air and roared again, until everyone's ears throbbed. *"Only get them out of it!"*

"Yes, Dad," said Martin.

Seven

Five minutes later, they were all sitting stiffly in a small, clean sitting room, and Mrs. Taylor was setting out tea things on several little round tables. She would not let Jess help, nor Frankie and Jenny. For some reason, she seemed to think that the two Adams girls were Jess's sisters.

"Aren't they sweet!" she said. "You must feel like a little mother to them."

"Not quite, really," Jess said, while Frankie and Jenny sat side by side on a sofa like two fierce mice and glared from Jess to Mrs. Taylor.

"I *love* little girls!" said Mrs. Taylor. "I've always wanted one of my own. I make a lot of fuss of Vernon's little sisters. Don't you think they're sweet?"

"Yes," said Jess, and Vernon wriggled rather.

Mrs. Taylor, perhaps because she liked girls so much, was a little sharp with the boys. She told Martin not to fidget and Vernon to mind his feet against the table. She asked Frank whether his hands were clean. Frank's hands, unfortunately, after searching the stables, were very grimy indeed. Martin was sent to show Frank where to wash. Jess sat on her hands, because there was still toffee on them, which had somehow collected a great deal of dirt, and was afraid that the next half hour was going to be rather trying. To her intense relief, just as Martin and Frank came soberly back, Mrs. Taylor was called away to see to something else, and they were left to have tea by themselves.

"Sorry," said Martin. "My people are sometimes rather a pain."

"Gave us tea, though," Vernon said consolingly, and began to pour it out.

Frankie and Jenny were still rather stormy. Frankie announced that neither of them were sweet, and Jenny added that they did not want any tea.

Vernon sighed. "You go without, then," he said. "I don't think you're sweet."

As this did not seem to soothe Frankie and Jenny, Jess tried. The only thing she could think of was to explain properly about Silas and the tooth, what Biddy had said about the heirloom, and what it seemed Buster had done. To her relief, it worked. Before she was halfway through the explanation, Frankie, not thinking what she was doing, reached out and picked up a sandwich. Vernon winked at Frank and put a cup of tea beside each of them. While Jess explained the nine tailors, Jenny picked up her cup and drank it down, looking at Jess all the time. Then she passed it to Vernon for more. Martin nearly spat his tea out, trying not to laugh. By the time Jess had finished, Frankie, too, was sipping her tea.

"So you do see," Jess said, "the only way we can cure Jenny and Silas seems to be to find the necklace. So could you tell us more about it, please?"

Jenny looked at her refilled teacup as if it astonished her. Then she looked at Vernon, rather accusingly, and Vernon tried not to laugh.

"Biddy *is* horrible," Jenny said. "I like Silas. He helps me with my sums."

"They're in the same class," Frankie explained to Jess.

"I bet you get a whole heap wrong, then," Vernon said.

"Yes," said Jenny, "but if he didn't help me, I'd get them *all* wrong. Only we don't know any more about the heirloom than we've said."

96

"I bet you do," Martin and Frank said together.

"It's you just being little kids," Vernon explained. "You say one thing, and you think we know the rest—like Silas." Frankie's chin went up. Vernon said hurriedly, "I'll show you. Ask you questions, and you'll see. When did you last see this necklace?"

"On Mother's dressing table," said Jenny.

"She used to let us sit on the stool and show us the things," said Frankie. "She showed Jenny hers, and she showed me mine. Mine's diamonds."

"There were lots of other things, too," said Jenny. "They all went."

"You see?" said Vernon. "You didn't say that before. Where was this dressing table?"

"In the big room at the front, upstairs," said Frankie.

"You mean, in this house?" asked Martin.

The two girls nodded. "We told you. We lived here," said Frankie. "It's our house really."

"And when did they go?" Jess asked.

Frankie and Jenny looked at each other. "After Mother went," said Jenny. "Mother went when we lived here, before the money went."

"You mean she died?" Vernon asked, rather tactlessly, Jess thought.

They both shook their heads indignantly. "No. She just went. We told you."

Jess made faces at Vernon.

Vernon said, "Someone told them that, I bet, not to upset them. And when did the necklaces and things go?" he asked.

"After we moved to the Mill House," said Jenny. "We heard Aunt saying."

"You're sure they weren't sold?" asked Frank.

"No, they weren't," said Frankie, "because they were too precious. But we know Biddy did it, because we heard Aunt say it was after she'd been once. They had the police."

"So it was at *your* house!" said Frank. "If you'd told us properly, we needn't have wasted our time looking here. Have you looked in your house?"

"Not really," said Jenny. "We thought they'd be here."

"Why?" said Martin.

"They're little kids. They don't think clear," Vernon explained.

"Because Biddy used to come here a lot, when we lived here," Jenny said. "But we've been all over everywhere here, lots of times."

"You're telling me you have!" said Martin. "But I don't think they're here. Do you?"

"No," said Frankie. "We'd better look in our house."

"Not unless there's us there," said Vernon. "Under-

98

stand? If Biddy's found out, then she's going to send Buster's lot to stop you as soon as you start. So you've got to wait until we're there to hold them off while you look. We'll get ourselves painted, and you can search while we're sitting there tomorrow."

Frank made a face and groaned. "Isn't there some easier way?" he said. "Or do you *have* to make it as boring as possible?"

"It's not boring," said Vernon cheerfully. "It's a good way to do it."

"Unless the Aunt or Mr. Adams go and tell Biddy we're looking," said Jess. "Frankie— No. Not you, Frank. *Frankie.*"

"Can't we call you Fanny?" Frank said to Frankie. "It's muddling. I keep thinking they mean me."

"So do I," said Frankie, "but I'm not going to be Fanny all the same. It's what they shout."

"Be Frances, then," said Jess, "and listen, anyway. Did your father give himself to Biddy like Buster? Or did your aunt? Because, if they did, it's awfully horrid and dangerous to do what Vernon wants."

"I don't think so," said Frankie. "We were too little to know much, but we think it was gradual. She sort of got them bit by bit, and I don't think they *like* doing what she wants. They just have to."

"And it makes them all funny," said Jenny. "Not sensible. Sort of sleepy."

"Really?" said Frank unbelievingly. "Your aunt, too, as well as your father?"

"They're just imagining it," Martin said. "I bet the Aunt's been that way peculiar all her life."

"No, we're not," said Jenny. "She's got them. Really." True or not, it was easy to see both little girls believed it.

Jess, Frank, and Martin all found it next to impossible to believe. Jess felt it must be true, about Mr. Adams at least, because of the way Buster's gang had appeared and chased them, but Frank and Martin thought even that must have been an accident. Vernon was the only one who seemed to believe what Jenny said, and it made not the slightest difference to his plan. Silas was his brother, and, anyway, he liked being painted.

Once again, they all found themselves doing what Vernon said. They arranged to meet at the Mill House at ten the next morning, and Frankie and Jenny agreed to hunt for heirlooms while the others sat for the Aunt. After this, they thanked Mrs. Taylor for the tea and tried to leave.

Mrs. Taylor insisted on kissing Frankie and Jenny before she let them go. Jess and Frank left her hugging them, and the little girls glaring, and scurried away to their bicycles.

"What's the hurry?" said Frank, who had hoped to spend a little longer with Martin, whom he was coming rather to like.

"Bridge Street," said Jess. "We must, Frank. And I'd rather die than be kissed by Mrs. Taylor, wouldn't you?"

"She wouldn't kiss me even if I offered to let her," said Frank. "What's she got against boys, anyway? You'd think only girls were human, the way she goes on."

"Count yourself lucky," said Jess. "You're free from passionate kisses, at least."

Frank continued to grumble, however, until Jess remembered the strange lady guest and the Eyes. She told Frank about it, to sweeten his temper. Frank was so impressed that he nearly fell off his bicycle. He had to turn into the curb and stop.

"*That's* what it was!" he said. "That's what came over Buster! I couldn't think what got into him. Nor could he, either. How splendid! It's like having a secret weapon."

"You mean the Eyes?" said Jess. "Really? You mean they worked?"

"Of course they did!" shouted Frank. The whole street rang. "They warded off evil. Don't tell me Buster's not evil."

Jess supposed he was. Certainly he was, if he belonged to Biddy. She and Frank pedaled on toward Bridge Street and Jess thought about it most of the way. If this was true, then they really did have a sort of secret weapon—but, at the same time, it made it all much more serious. Real evil. The lady had meant what she said, even though she was mad and intense.

Frank interrupted by saying, "What do you think of Martin? I rather like him."

"Yes," said Jess. "But I like Vernon better."

"Trust you to be different," said Frank.

"But I do," said Jess, catching up with the conversation and discovering she meant what she said. "Martin's just a follower. He does what you say. You like him because you like ordering people about."

"I like that from *you!*" said Frank. They would have had a bitter argument if they had not, at that moment, reached Bridge Street. It seemed to be empty, apart from everyone's dustbins left out to be collected, and one small boy sitting gloomily in a go-cart outside the pub on the corner.

"I bet they're still out," said Frank. They left their bicycles at the curb and went over to the narrow front door of Number 2. "Your turn to knock," said Frank to Jess.

Jess went up the two steps. She had her hand on the knocker when the small boy in the go-cart looked up and saw them. "Here!" he said.

"What do you mean?" said Frank. "There's nothing wrong in knocking at a door."

"No, it's me wants you," said the boy. "Come on over."

Jess let the knocker go, gently, so as not to let it knock, and they walked rather suspiciously over to the small boy. He seemed too small to count, somehow. He was very dirty. His nose was running, and there were tear marks down his filthy face. As they came up, he wiped his nose on his sleeve, which, as Jess said afterward, was a dreadful habit, but she supposed he had no handkerchief.

"That was my letter," he said. "But I been out with Mum. And you was out all day. I went back to your shed."

"I know. I'm sorry," said Jess. "We did call after lunch, when you were out. What's your name? Are you desprit?"

"Don't I look like it?" said the small boy. "I'm Kevin, I am."

Frank remembered him. Last time he had seen Kevin, he was being pulled across the river, probably in this same go-cart, on the way to see Biddy. He had not been at the hut this morning, though. He was the very smallest one in the gang, and Frank rather thought he was Stafford's youngest brother. "You're in Buster's gang, then," he said.

"I were," said Kevin. "Until he gone mad and give them to Biddy Iremonger."

"Not you, though?" Frank asked.

"*Not* me," said Kevin, with great feeling. "I was dead scared. The half of us were all dead scared. But he got the big ones to go in with him. She got nine of them."

"We know," said Jess. "What did you want us for?"

"To get 'em back," said Kevin. "You *got* to. There's Stafford going funny in the head with it, and old Ray got the shakes all night, but they can't do nothing because Buster give 'em away. And this afternoon, we was out shopping with Mum, and there came a whistle, sort of, and Stafford and Ray just gone and vanished. Mum was real upset." At the memory, tears began to run out of Kevin's eyes again. Some went down the white tracks left for them, others made themselves new ones, and he snuffled. "I had to say they was okay," he said. "And I didn't know *where* they was."

Jess could not help feeling sorry for him. "But if they gave themselves," she said as kindly as she could, "I can't see what *we* can do."

"Think of something," Kevin begged them. "You said difficult tasks, and if you can get a tooth out of Vernon Wilkins, you can do anything."

"Except it wasn't Vernon's," said Frank. "It belonged to Silas."

Being told of this deception upset Kevin even more. The tears ran so fast from his eyes that his face was nearly cleaned by them. "Oh, slime it!" he said. "Cor degutting darn it! Then Silas got face-ache."

"He's got a face about three sizes too big," said Frank. "And he's ill."

"He stick up for me in the playground," said Kevin miserably. "I don't like to think it's Silas got it. See here. You get that tooth back so as Stafford and Ray belong to their own selves again, and I'll give you five pence. I got one. Mum give it me to get sweets with for not vanishing, too." To prove he had the money, Kevin showed them, folded in his grimy hand, a white new coin.

Jess and Frank looked at it longingly. "Can we?" said Frank.

"No," said Jess, remembering what the lady had said. "We're under contract to get the tooth back, anyway."

"But not to get Buster," said Frank.

"I think it would be a bad act disguised as a good one," said Jess, "if we took money for it. Don't you think so, Kevin?"

"Not if you get 'em back," said Kevin. "I'd give you more than five pence to do that, if I got it."

"We ought," said Jess piously, "to do it as a good deed, to balance all our bad ones."

"How *can* we do it, anyway?" said Frank. "And if he wants to give us the money, why not let him?"

"I'll save it," Kevin suggested. "If you get 'em back, I'll give it you for a reward, like the newspapers."

"That's it," said Frank. "We owe it to Vernon. It's not for us."

"Well, mind you don't lose it or spend it," said Jess, weakening.

"I won't. Promise," said Kevin. "And you *will* try to do it, will you?"

"We'll try," said Frank. "But we ought to warn you we may not manage it. We'll have the gang themselves trying to stop us, now they belong to Biddy, you see."

Kevin grinned. "I bet you do it," he said. "You always got good ideas. Even Buster says so."

With this to encourage them, Frank and Jess got on their bicycles and pedaled off home.

"It's all very well to be holy," said Frank, "but this isn't an Own Back, Jess. He's scared stiff and miserable, and it's not even for him, really."

"That's just temptation," said Jess. "And you oughtn't to get delivered to it, Frank, like a parcel or something. We should do it to help him, out of the kindness of our hearts."

"What about the kindness of *his* heart?" said Frank. "If he wants to give us five pence out of it, *I'm* not going to stop him."

I am, thought Jess. Secretly, she had decided that the whole thing was too big and dangerous for them. If Biddy could whisk people away from shopping with their mothers to chase other people through games of croquet, and if she could do this because she had at least one grown-up and possibly two in her power, then she must be a very strong witch indeed. Jess felt it was time she and Frank became Limited. She decided to try to make their parents understand.

"Mummy," she said, that evening, "suppose Biddy Iremonger really *was* a witch. What would we do?"

"Nothing, of course," said Mrs. Pirie. "There is no such thing as witches."

"There *are*," said Jess. "And I think Biddy *is*. I know four things she did."

"Jess!" said her mother. "Biddy is a poor old lady, a bit mad, and very well educated indeed. She knows Greek."

"And magic," said Jess. "Bad magic, Mummy."

Mr. Pirie suddenly rose out of his chair. "Jessica, that's enough! If I catch you talking like that again, I'll stop your pocket money till Christmas."

Jess had to stop, partly because of the threat and partly because it was plainly no good trying to convince her parents. So, before she went to bed, she caught Frank and gave him the little brown Eye.

"There," she said. "That's all I can think of. If we keep together, we'll both be protected. Thread it on your tiepin

and wear it. I'll wear my bracelet, with the blue Eye on it."
She made sure Frank did as she told him, then and there.

"Who did you say liked ordering people about?" said
Frank.

"Vernon Wilkins," said Jess, and went to bed.

Eight

The next morning, before they set off for the Mill House, Frank asked Jess if she had put up the CLOSED FOR GOOD notice.

"Oh, good heavens!" said Jess. "Not yet. And I do want it up, because it looks as if it says we closed because we want to do good in future."

"It could just as well mean we only do bad things," Frank objected as he followed Jess down the garden. "Why not just take down the first notice?"

"Not yet," said Jess. "It *was* such a good idea. I want everyone to know."

"There's someone knowing now," said Frank, as they reached the shed.

Sure enough, someone was outside the window, reading the notice. When they got near enough, they saw, to their surprise, that it was Mr. Adams. He was laughing, in a dreamy sort of way, as if the notice amused him.

"Good morning," he called through the glass.

Jess politely opened the window and said "Good morning" back. But, she thought, if he wants to be a customer, we'll just have to say we're closed.

"I've got a message for you two," said Mr. Adams, "but I can't for the life of me remember what it was."

"From Frankie and Jenny?" suggested Frank. Mr. Adams really was the most absentminded-looking person he had ever seen. It did not surprise him at all that he had forgotten the message.

"No," said Mr. Adams. "It wasn't them."

"Your aunt," said Jess. "I mean—er—Miss Adams, is she? She wants to paint us."

"Probably," said Mr. Adams. "I know she's expecting you, so it must be. Perhaps if we walk down together the message will come back to me."

A little shyly, Frank and Jess let themselves out into the allotment path and walked along beside Mr. Adams. He seemed, as Jess said, to be a nice man, but he was so vague that he rather alarmed them. He said suddenly, "Her name's Mrs. Andrews. She's a widow." And they had not the faintest idea what he meant at first.

"You mean your aunt?" Frank asked.

"She's my sister," said Mr. Adams. "She wants to paint you." As he said this, he opened the gate into the allotments, to go down the path.

"And Vernon and Martin," said Jess. "It's much *nicer* by the road."

"But this way's shorter," said Mr. Adams. "Come on."

They felt they had to follow him, even though it meant going past Biddy's hut. Jess had a sudden horrible suspicion. Suppose Mr. Adams had come to lure them into Biddy's clutches? The idea made her shake in her shoes, until she remembered the way Buster had been driven off by the two Eyes. If Mr. Adams had been evil, he would not have been able to walk so near them. And, remembering the Eyes, Jess felt better, because—surely— they would protect her and Frank from Biddy. All the same, she would have given a great deal not to have to go this way with someone supposed to be in Biddy's power.

Frank felt the same, although he thought he did not believe Mr. Adams was in anyone's power. His feelings came out when he asked, rather rudely to Jess's mind, "Why aren't you at work, like everyone else?"

"I'm on holiday," said Mr. Adams. "Like you. I'm a teacher, you see, and you wouldn't deny me the holidays you get, would you?"

"Oh, no," said Frank, rather thinking he would if he could.

They squeezed round the neglected fence and walked among the rubbish and the muggy smell. When they got to the big bramble bush, Jess was holding her breath with nervousness. But Mr. Adams went on calmly following the path, where it took a big bend away from Biddy's hut and twisted through a heap of broken bicycles. When they were opposite Biddy's hut, Mr. Adams jumped, as if he had trodden on a prickle.

"Of course!" he said. "I remember now. The message was from Miss Iremonger. She says you are to stop searching."

Frank said, very loudly, hoping Biddy would overhear: "That's all right. We *have* stopped searching."

"For the moment," Jess added, in a mutter, for the sake of truthfulness.

"And what were you supposed to be looking for?" Mr. Adams asked politely.

"Er . . ." said Frank, wondering if Biddy could hear still, ". . . er . . . the root of all evil."

"Money, you mean?" said Mr. Adams.

"Sort of," Jess answered. Jewels, she supposed, were the next thing to money.

They followed Mr. Adams down to the bridge, under the bare willows, past the sprouting flags, and out across the planks. Mr. Adams said, "They may say money is the root of all evil, but it always strikes me as the root of most other things as well. I could do with more, whatever they call it. Couldn't you?"

"Yes," said Frank and Jess devoutly.

Mr. Adams reached the end of the bridge and turned to face them. "Is that why you put up that notice?" he asked.

Jess and Frank stopped in the middle of the bridge, feeling rather frightened. Mr. Adams was blocking one end. If they went back, there would be Biddy. They could not understand why he should be asking, unless Biddy had told him to find out more about Own Back.

"Yes," said Jess. "We'd less than no money, you see."

"We owed ten pence," said Frank.

Mr. Adams laughed and wandered dreamily out into the field. Frank and Jess ran over the rest of the bridge in order to reach the field before he remembered to block their way again. But Mr. Adams did not try to stop them. He waited for them to catch up, and then he said, "It's rather a good idea." Jess gave Frank a proud smile. "Yes," said Mr. Adams, "in the days of witchcraft, people would take such matters to a witch." Jess stopped smiling and put her hand on Frank's arm. "These days," said Mr. Adams, "there's no one to arrange revenge. You ought to do a roaring trade. May I ask what made you so hard up? I seem to be the kind of person who repels money—it goes whatever I do. Are you the same?"

"Not quite," said Frank.

"A chair broke, you see," Jess explained, "and our pocket money was stopped."

"I see," said Mr. Adams. They were nearly at the Mill House. As Mr. Adams spoke, they saw Martin and Vernon come round the side of the house and stand waiting for them by the door. "The other sitters?" Mr. Adams asked. Frank and Jess nodded. "It occurs to me," said Mr. Adams, suddenly sounding a good deal less dreamy, "that by painting your portraits my sister is probably depriving you of a morning's earning for Own Back Ltd."

"Not really," said Jess, because she was not at all sure that this was true. For one thing, there were no earnings. For another, they were being painted directly on Own Back business.

Mr. Adams obviously thought she was just being polite. "It seems rather hard luck," he said. Maybe the milkman had made a fuss, Frank thought, the time the Aunt caught and painted him. At any rate, Mr. Adams went on, "I've rather a conscience about it. Did you know that professional models always charge a fee for being painted?"

Frank said he had heard that they did, and watched hopefully, as Mr. Adams stood still and sorted vaguely in his pockets. Jess nudged Frank, and, when that did no good, trod on his toe, but Frank took no notice. It was worth it. Mr. Adams took his hand out of the fourth pocket he tried, holding a coin. It looked like five pence.

"This is all I can find," he said. "Will this do for a fee?"

Frank put out his hand to it. Jess jumped on his foot and said, "No! No, Frank. I mean, I don't want to be rude, but aren't you buying us off with this, Mr. Adams?"

Mr. Adams looked utterly astonished. It was not pretend astonishment, which makes grown-ups say things like "My dear child!" but real, deep-down amazement. It was plain he just had no idea what Jess was talking of, and no idea what to answer. Frank seized the moment, while Mr. Adams and Jess stared at each other, to take the money from Mr. Adams and his foot from under Jess's shoe.

"Do shut up, Jess," he said.

"I really don't understand," said Mr. Adams.

Jess would not let it rest. She pointed to Frank putting the five pence in his pocket. "Has he," she asked, "just done a bad deed disguised as a good one?"

"Not that I know of," said Mr. Adams. "Where did you get that idea?"

"A lady called Jessica," said Jess. "She—"

"Oh, a quotation," said Mr. Adams, laughing rather uncomfortably. "I think your friends are waiting. Where was this lady?"

"The big house on the London Road," said Jess. "Frankie says it was yours."

"Frankie," said Mr. Adams, "talks a great deal of nonsense. But we did live there once, for a while. That's true."

Vernon and Martin were becoming impatient. Vernon called out, "Are you staying all day, or shall we knock now?"

"Knock away," Mr. Adams called back, and without saying anything more, he went wandering away toward the bushy garden of the cheese-colored house.

Frank and Jess went to the door, while Vernon knocked. The Aunt, just as usual, arrived with a wagging cigarette and paint all over her.

"Oh," she said. "You came. I never thought you would. No blood, though. Can't you manage any today? Just a little?"

Martin looked at Vernon. "I know just where to hit you," he said. "I could make it bleed if you want."

Vernon did not want, and looked rather fierce about it.

"Not to worry," said the Aunt. "I can remember it quite well." Then she led the way to her painting room, and the four of them followed. Frankie and Jenny were standing at the door of their playroom. They looked at Vernon. Vernon nodded. Frankie and Jenny replied each with a fierce little nod and went hurrying away.

There began, as far as Frank was concerned, another time as maddening as the first. They had to sit there, talking of this and that, so that the Aunt would not guess what was going on, listening to Frankie and Jenny ransacking the house. Frank longed to help them. He knew it would be more fun than being painted, and he was dying to make sure they looked everywhere. From the sound of it, they were being very thorough, but he wanted to make sure. He could attend to nothing but their scufflings and thumpings. He strained his ears for them and wondered what each noise meant. Then came a terrific crashing from somewhere near that even the Aunt wondered about. She raised her eyebrows.

"All the saucepans," she said. "What are those kids up to now?"

"Getting dinner?" Vernon suggested.

"Yes," said Jess. "And you reach for the little saucepan at the top to do the scrambled eggs in, and you reach and you reach, and suddenly the whole pile goes down."

"Don't think there *are* any eggs," said the Aunt.

"Spinach, then," Jess said, hectically. "The big saucepan from the bottom of the pile. Pull that out and they all fall over."

"No spinach," said the Aunt.

"Spinach," said Vernon, "is very good for you."

"But," said Martin, "it goes down to nothing when you cook it."

"A big saucepan full of nothing, then," Jess said brightly.

"That's what it sounded like," said the Aunt. "About a hundred big saucepans full of nothing. Stop jigging, you lot."

They hastily sat as still as they could and listened while the search progressed round the rest of the house. There was a sound like books or boxes being thrown around, rattlings, trailings, and then slow, hollow thumping as the two little girls went upstairs, testing and searching each step as they went. After that, the search became rather more distant until, suddenly, they heard Jenny's uneven feet treading across the ceiling. They all looked up, without meaning to.

"Look in front," said the Aunt. Then she shouted, startlingly loudly, "Jenny! Get out of my bedroom. There's a wet canvas there."

There was a long silence from overhead. Jess, Frank, Vernon, and Martin looked straight ahead at the Aunt and knew that Jenny was still there. After a while, they heard a careful shuffle, then another. Frank held his breath. But the Aunt painted busily and did not seem to hear.

"The weather's improving," Jess said wildly. "Going from bad to worse beautifully, don't you think?"

"Sure," said the Aunt. "Tornadoes any day now."

"And all the roots are budding," said Jess.

"Potatoes upward," said the Aunt.

Frank kicked Jess and was heartily glad when he heard a door softly close overhead.

Then there was a time when none of them could tell what Frankie and Jenny were up to, followed by complete silence. After that, they suddenly heard them talking, somewhere outside by the window.

"There's a big clump of grass, Jenny. Help me pull it up."

There was a pause. Then Jenny said, "I don't like wood lice."

Frank could not think what they were doing, until he heard their feet clattering on wood. Then he realized that they were on the big mill wheel, searching it slat by slat. He thought it was clever of them to have thought of that. It sounded fun, too. Their voices gradually came from higher and higher up, until they seemed to be right at the top of the wheel.

"Jenny!" called Frankie. "I've found a nest of mice! Come and see. Ten baby mice."

Jenny's irregular feet climbed past the wall. For a second, the models thought Frankie was pretending mice and meaning necklaces. But it seemed not. Jenny gave a little shriek. "Don't let them run on me, Frankie!" Then they heard scutterings, and Jenny climbing down again, very fast.

"Don't be a baby," Frankie shouted.

"Mice," said Vernon. "Funny, girls being afraid of mice."

"I'm not," said Jess.

"Kate Matthews is, though," said Martin.

"Jess is scared of worms," Frank said.

"Silly girl," said the Aunt. "Would you all stop craning your heads? Go and catch the mice afterward, if you want. They're just vermin."

Then there were noises outside, quite indescribable. A scraping and a crunching, and distant feet. Most unexpectedly, a piece of iron pipe dived past the window. Vernon winced.

"Gutter!" he whispered.

Frankie, it seemed, was up on the roof now. The little girls were being very thorough indeed. Jenny seemed to be halfway up the mill wheel, calling instructions.

"Frankie, if you grab that piece of wall on the left—no, I mean right—no, *right*, Frankie. Then you can pull up on the chimney."

There were uncertain, clattering, faraway footsteps. A piece of slate dived past the window, followed by what looked like a chimneypot.

"Be careful!" called Jenny.

All four models began talking hard.

"I always think," said Jess, "that Wee Willie Winkie must have been a dreadful nuisance."

"Last time we had the sweep," said Martin, "he came in a white coat. And he was clean."

"We lost six slates last month, in the wind," said Frank.

"When I fell off our roof," said Vernon, "I had to have stitches."

They were interrupted by a long, sliding rumble. Slates began raining past the window. Jenny was screaming instructions.

"Drat those kids!" said the Aunt. "What *are* they up to?"

The rain of slates stopped. There was a slow slithering. The models could almost feel Frankie sliding down the roof. Any moment, they expected her to dive past the window, too. Then they heard Mr. Adams shouting.

"Frankie! Get *down*! Get down this minute. Jenny, get off the wheel. It's quite rotten. Get *down*, Frankie."

Very distantly, Frankie said, "I can't."

It was too much to bear. Vernon said, "Can we go and help her?"

"You sit where you are," said the Aunt. "He'll cope."

They had to listen to Mr. Adams coping. They saw a ladder go past the window and heard it thump against the wall. They heard it being climbed. Mr. Adams was saying, "What is she doing up there, anyway?"

Jenny answered from much lower down. "She's looking for something I've lost."

"Oh, is she?" said Mr. Adams. "Well, it'll have to stay lost."

They could not help exchanging glances at that. They listened to more thumping and watched another slate dive past the window. Then they heard the ladder and the voices going away. For a while, there was no noise at all.

"Praised be!" said the Aunt. "Maybe you'll sit still now."

They were doing their best to sit still, when the door was flung open and Frankie stood in the doorway, very grimy, with her apron in ribbons. "Aunt," she said.

"What is it *now?*" said the Aunt. "Go away."

Frankie, however, was looking at Frank and Jess, not at the Aunt. "I just came to say," she said, "that Father's gone for a walk. He went down to the river."

"What if he has?" said the Aunt. "Why do you have to tell *me?*"

Frankie, staring significantly at Vernon, answered, "I just thought he'd be late for lunch if you let him go now."

"Frankie," said the Aunt, "go away, or I'll paint you in stripes."

Nine

The next twenty minutes were almost unbearable. They sat helplessly in front of the Aunt, knowing that every minute made it more certain Biddy knew they were still searching, and quite unable to get away. Jess suggested twice to the Aunt that it was lunchtime and they ought to go, but all the Aunt said was, "Won't be five minutes."

"No," muttered Frank. "You'll be half an hour instead." And they all knew that this would allow plenty of time for Biddy to summon Buster and the other eight. They felt completely trapped. Jess gave up suggesting it was time to go, and they all, instead, concentrated on being kept there as long as possible. At least they were safe inside the Mill House, even if they were late for lunch. Everyone wriggled and jigged and tried to interrupt the Aunt as much as they could.

"What's the matter?" asked the Aunt. "Got a flea?"

"Crick in the neck," said Vernon.

"Could we stretch our legs for a minute, please?" Martin asked.

The Aunt looked at her watch. Then she popped her cigarette into the paint pot. "Okay," she said. "You win. I can see you want to be off. We'll call it a day."

Jess was almost sure she looked at her watch to see if she had given Biddy time to be ready for them. She could see that Vernon thought so, too. None of them had the heart to be very interested in the painting. They crowded round it politely, and the Aunt told them it still needed working up. To Frank's mind, it looked just the same as before, only thicker.

"Very nice," said Martin, trying to be hearty. "I wouldn't know that was me."

"It isn't," said the Aunt. "That's you on the other side."

Martin said, "Oh!" rather blankly, and they were all very glad when the Aunt wandered out of the room to the kitchen, calling over her shoulder to them to let themselves out.

"What shall we do?" Frank said rather hopelessly.

The playroom door opened and Jenny put her head out, looking whiter and fiercer than they had ever seen her. "Come in here," she said. When they had all trooped in, she said, "Now do you believe me? He's told on *us* now." Jess suddenly realized how it must feel when you could not trust your own father. She felt quite shocked by the idea, and then, after a second, very angry—angry because of Jenny, and angry because of Mr. Adams, too, who she knew was a nice man, left to himself.

"Are you sure he has?" Martin asked.

"Take a look," said Frankie, who was beside the window.

They looked. If they bent their heads sideways, they could see round the big mill wheel into the bushy garden. They were just in time to see Stafford dodge back behind a flowering currant. After that, not even Frank and Martin doubted in the slightest that Mr. Adams had indeed told Biddy they were searching for the necklace. No one doubted Frankie when she told them that Buster was in the field outside the front door with four more of the gang. It gave them the most peculiar feeling. It was like being besieged, Frank supposed, with traitors inside the castle, but it did not feel like that in the least. It felt worrying and hopeless, and not at all exciting. Martin put it best when he said, "I'm going to get into trouble if I'm late for lunch."

"We have to go," Vernon agreed.

"Back or front way?" asked Frank.

"Front's open," said Vernon. "We can run."

Vernon seemed to be right, but Jess was worried about the little girls. "What about them?" she asked him.

"We'll stay indoors," said Frankie. "We'll be all right."

"But don't budge out," said Vernon. "They'll be after you, if we get by."

"And what about the necklace?" Jenny asked dolefully. "We've looked everywhere except on the roof."

"No, you haven't," said Vernon. "No one searched the painting room. It must be there somewhere."

"Oh, how silly!" said Jess. "And no one *can* look there, if it's being used for painting all the time."

"She's not always there," said Jenny. "We'll look when she's out."

"No, you won't," said Vernon. "You look when *we're* here. We'll come back this afternoon and get her talking. You look then. How do you think you'll manage against two grown-ups and a whole gang of boys?"

Jenny and Frankie looked fierce and did not answer.

"He's right," said Jess. "Do wait till we're here."

"We know," said Frankie.

Then there seemed nothing for it but to try to get through the gang outside. Everyone took a deep breath. Then Frank, either because his last hour had come, or because he wanted to put his last hour off a little—he was not sure which—took out of his pocket the five pence Mr. Adams had given him and passed it to Vernon.

"Here you are," he said. "Here's what we owe you."

Then Jess remembered she had Vernon's fifty pence still, and gave that back to him, too.

Vernon was pleased. "I meant to ask you," he said. "There's a car Silas wants, costs forty-five."

"Oh, let's *go!*" Martin said irritably.

So they went. They threw open the front door and tried to make a dash for it, round the Mill House to the road. But it was no good. Buster and the other four rose out of the grass almost at their feet, with air guns and peashooters. Bullets rattled, all shapes and sizes, and most of them hit their targets. Buster shouted. They heard Stafford answer from the garden, and heavy crashings as the rest of the gang hurried through the bushes to help their leader.

"*Run!*" yelled Vernon. He and Martin made off with their heads down.

"After 'em!" roared Buster.

Jess snatched Frank's arm as he tried to follow Martin and Vernon. "Let go!" said Frank.

"No, you fool! Cover their retreat," said Jess, and she swung Frank round and pushed him straight at Buster. All

Frank could do was to put his arms over his face against the bullets and wonder which to kick: Jess or Buster. He decided to kick Buster and landed out blindly with one foot. Buster was out of reach. Jess pushed Frank onward. Frank took his arms down and saw that Buster was backing away, with his face twisted up. Stafford and his party, looking puzzled and indignant, were backing away, too, toward the garden. On the other side, Frank saw Vernon and Martin almost at the road. He and Jess were alone inside a ring of nine angry boys, who all seemed to be backing away from them.

"You done it again," complained Buster. "What do you keep *doing?*"

"That would be telling," said Jess. "But you might as well go away. You're not going to be able to touch us."

"Zombie-parts-pancake Piries!" said Buster. "That's what *you* think!"

"I'll show you," said Jess. "Come on, Frank." And she yanked Frank a step or so in Buster's direction. To Frank's delight, the whole gang immediately backed away again, swearing horribly, as if he and Jess were armed with prickles. One boy shouted to them to stop. All of them looked angry and puzzled.

"Why is it?" said Frank.

"Eyes!" said Jess. "Come on." And she advanced again.

Frank grinned as the gang hastily gave back another step. He could not see why the little Eyes should work, but it was plain that they did. Buster and the rest were very uncomfortable indeed. Frank could have kicked himself this time for not remembering their secret weapon. In the distance, Frank saw Martin mount his pony and Vernon climb on a huge, rusty bicycle. Jess saw them, too, and stopped.

"See?" she said. "Now you just leave us alone."

"I'm maggot-slime disemboweled if I will," said Buster.

It seemed to be deadlock. Jess and Frank stood under the walls of the house. The gang stood all round them, glowering. Martin and Vernon, meanwhile, made their getaway down the road. Frank supposed he ought to be thankful, but he was not. He could have done with their support. And there they stayed, for several long, long minutes, until Frankie suddenly altered things by leaning out of the Aunt's bedroom window. Jess said afterward that she ought to have poured boiling oil—or at least cold water—on the gang's heads. Frank pointed out that it would have hit them, too.

What Frankie did was to shout, "Leave them alone, you great ugly cowards!"

The gang looked up. "Sweet slime-guts Fanny Adams!" jeered Squeaky Voice.

"Get her!" said one of the others.

Stafford's brother Ray pointed his air gun and fired. Frankie ducked down. There was a splintering crack, and several pieces of glass fell down onto the grass, leaving a white starry hole in the window.

"Curried-bowel nit!" said Stafford to Ray.

There was a very difficult silence. The gang, instead of just standing, were standing ready to run, glaring accusingly at Frank and Jess. Frank and Jess looked accusingly back. Frankie seemed to have gone. The house was quiet as the grave.

At length, Buster said to Frank, "Now look what you made us do!"

"*Made* you!" said Frank. "Made you dance a hornpipe!"

Everyone looked uneasily up at the broken window again. One or two of the gang began to back away. Jess thought that, with luck, she could have them on the run in a second or so.

"Frankie's gone to tell," she said. "You'd better go."

It was clear that there was nothing the gang would have liked better to do. But for some reason they did not.

"You got to come, too," said Buster. "Prisoners. We caught you."

"I like that!" said Frank. "If we're prisoners, you're Julius Caesar."

"You *got* to come," repeated Buster.

131

"He may *be* Julius Caesar," said Jess. "His face *is* rather like a lemon squeezer, don't you think, Frank?"

"But we're not prisoners," said Frank. "You just try."

All Buster could do was glower and snuffle through his nose. The gang was all round the Piries, but none of the nine seemed to be able to come nearer than three feet away.

"You *got* to," said Buster, rather desperately, glancing at the house and forgetting to swear in his hurry.

"We've got to go home to lunch," said Jess, "and there's nothing you can do to stop us, Buster Knell. So there!" She took hold of Frank's arm and set off, very firmly, toward the road. The nearest boys backed away as soon as she moved. Jess simply went on walking, pulling Frank, and all the gang could do was to close in round the Piries, about three feet off, and follow them, calling names. Neither Frank nor Jess liked being called names, but they put their heads in the air and went marching on, pretending to take no notice.

"You'll vampire-stomach well pay for this!" said Buster, for about the hundredth time.

"*You're* paying already," said Frank. "And I hope you frizzle and fry."

"What do you mean?" said Stafford.

"You know perfectly well," Jess retorted. "Slaves. And

you might think of how your mother feels next time you vanish, Stafford Briggs."

"You shut up!" said Stafford and Ray together. Jess thought they looked very uncomfortable.

"How do you know?" Buster demanded. "What's it got—"

Then, suddenly, the gang fell very quiet again, except that Squeaky Voice muttered, "Look out!"

Jess and Frank looked up and saw Mr. Adams wandering down the road toward them. He was so near that the gang had no time to get away. Nor had Jess and Frank, although Mr. Adams was the last person they felt they wanted to meet just then. Everyone stood still, while Mr. Adams came up to them, vaguely smiling.

"Hallo," he said. He seemed not to have the least notion that it was his doing that Jess and Frank were surrounded like this by Buster's gang.

Everyone said, "Hallo" in reply, the gang as well, in grudging mutters. Frank could see that the gang were all ready to run as soon as he or Jess told Mr. Adams about the broken window. Frank left it to Jess to tell. His feeling was that Mr. Adams deserved his window broken for going to Biddy.

Jess, however, felt the same as Frank. She was sure that Frankie or Jenny would tell Mr. Adams as soon as he got home, anyway. So, when Mr. Adams asked if the painting was finished, she said, "Yes," and added coldly, "but we have to be getting home to lunch now."

"Ah, yes," said Mr. Adams. "So have I." And he seemed about to walk on.

Frank decided that Buster and the gang ought not to get away with their crimes entirely. So he said, looking meaningly at Buster, "I think you ought to take care of Frankie and Jenny, Mr. Adams."

Buster gave himself away, by saying indignantly, "Hey! I ain't done nothing to them yet."

Mr. Adams did not seem to realize. "They've become friends of yours, have they?" he asked, meaning the gang as well as the Piries.

The gang looked sulky. Jess could have shaken Mr. Adams. "Yes," she said. "Very *great* friends, Mr. Adams. And you should look after them. You neglect them awfully, you know."

There was another broken-window kind of silence. Mr. Adams blinked at Jess, and Jess stared firmly back at him. The gang felt they had had enough and began to sneak away, past Mr. Adams, up the road. Frank wanted to go as well, but did not dare. He had to wait while Mr. Adams slowly decided what to say.

Then, oddly, Mr. Adams did not say anything at all.

He just gave a sort of nod, or a sort of head shake, toward Jess and went wandering on toward the Mill House. Frank and Jess stood by themselves in a road blessedly cleared of the gang.

"Jess," Frank said. "That was awful cheek."

"I know," said Jess. "And he deserved it. He *does* neglect them, you can see, and he knows he does. He deserves to have his window broken, too. I almost even think he deserves to be in Biddy's power."

"I don't know," Frank answered. "I'm beginning to think no one deserves that much. Look at Kevin. I hope we didn't give him away."

Ten

They did not meet the gang again, but they were very late for lunch. Mrs. Pirie was so cross that Frank and Jess were unable to rush out again straight afterward, much as they wanted to. They had to do the washing-up instead.

Jess sighed as she ran the hot water. "The injustice of it!" she said. "It's Mr. Adams's fault, and Biddy's, and Buster's, not ours at all. But I wouldn't mind if I only knew what Martin and Vernon were doing."

"Searching the paint pots, I hope," said Frank, looking with hatred at a stack of plates and a heap of saucepans beyond. "*I* wouldn't mind if there wasn't so *much* washing-up. I think Mummy feeds an army while we're not here to see. We never ate with all these spoons, I know."

"Maybe it's breakfast as well," Jess suggested, squirting washing-up liquid into the water. "Glasses first, Frank."

"All ten of them?" said Frank. "You see what I mean? There were only three of us."

"Perhaps Biddy did it to spite us," said Jess.

That was exactly what it felt like. They got grimly on with it, but as soon as they had cleared one stack of dirty plates, they found another, nestling behind that. It was just like an evil enchantment.

"Perhaps Mummy's in Biddy's power, too," said Frank.

"Oh, I hope *not!*" said Jess.

Frank pointed a bunch of spoons toward the window. "Look."

Jess looked. There was nothing but the garden, and the concrete path, and somebody's ugly old cat washing itself with one leg in the air. It was a very ugly cat, with its ears all chewed up. It was ginger and tabby and black and white—and Jess had a feeling she had seen it before.

"It's Biddy's," said Frank.

Jess felt a row of shivers chase one another down her back. "But it's just a cat," she said. "Throw a spoon at it, Frank. I would, only I'd miss."

"So would I miss," said Frank. "It's a witch's cat. Let's just take no notice."

"But *it's* noticing *us*," said Jess.

"A cat can look at a king," said Frank. "And it can't talk."

"How do we know it can't?" said Jess. With Biddy, she thought, anything was possible. She was sure the ugly creature had been sent to keep an eye on them and that, somehow, it would report to Biddy if it found them hunting for Jenny's heirloom again. "Oh," she said, "if it stays there, we'll *never* cure Silas. And I never even asked Vernon how Silas was."

"He'd have said if he was better," Frank said gloomily. Seeing that cat was like seeing failure staring them in the face. It was no good. Biddy was too strong and too cunning for them. He could not ever see them undoing the harm Own Back seemed to have done. But then, as soon as he reached that idea, Frank began to get angry. It all seemed to be Biddy's fault, really. All he and Jess had done was to get hold of a tooth in the kindest possible way. It was Biddy magicked it. And long before they had thought of Own Back, Biddy had been at work on the Adams family, making Jenny limp, hiding her necklace, and getting Mr. Adams and maybe the Aunt, too, in her power.

"I'm blowed if she'll get away with it!" said Frank. He

opened the window and hurled the whole handful of spoons at the cat.

None of them hit it. They just clattered down all over the path and the flower beds. But the cat ran for its life. Frank was delighted at the way it ran. It streaked up the garden like a rabbit, and he saw it scramble frantically over the fence beside the potting shed. Frank dusted his hands together and went triumphantly out to collect the spoons.

Jess, meanwhile, scrambled the rest of the dishes into the sink. By the time Frank came in with the spoons, she was nearly finished. She washed the spoons again, and they *were* finished.

Jess dried her hands. "What shall we do?" she asked. "Go to the Mill House? If Vernon and Martin were coming here, they'd have come by now."

"Yes," said Frank, wiping the spoons. "By the way, did we take down the Own Back notice, in the end?"

"Gracious, no!" Jess put her hands over her mouth. "I clean forgot. I didn't even put up the CLOSED notice, because Mr. Adams came. Oh, Frank! Suppose there's a queue of customers!"

"We'll send them away," said Frank. "I've done with it. Come on." He threw down the tea towel, and both of them ran through the garden to the shed.

To their relief, there was no one outside the window.

Jess hurried forward to get the notice in, and tripped over something in the way. She looked down to see what it was. It was a leg—a large, sturdy leg, in dirty blue denim, with a battered shoe on the end of it.

"Oh, Frank!" she said. "Come quick! There's a piece of a person here."

Jess backed away from the leg just as Frank ran forward. They collided. Frank staggered and trod on the leg.

"Sliced toes in puke!" said the leg. "Now you broke my ankle."

Frank and Jess, holding on to each other, and very shaken, leaned forward and looked into the space beyond the garden roller. Buster Knell was there. It was his leg, and it was joined onto him in the usual way—but he looked unusual all the same. He was bent over, hugging himself, and did not seem to want to move. Odder still, his eyes were swollen all round, and there were tear stains all over his face and wet new tears on his sweater. Frank and Jess stared. It was odd enough to have Buster in their shed, but even odder to see he had been crying his eyes out there. Frank was quite awed, because no one had ever before seen Buster cry. Jess was almost sorry for him.

"What *is* the matter?" she said.

Buster gave out language—slimy, degutted, maggot-puked, body-bits language—and, when he had finished doing that, he burst into tears again and said pathetically, "And I thought you weren't never coming, either."

"But why?" said Jess. "What is it?"

"Her," said Buster. "Look what she done to me."

"What?" said Frank. Apart from the tears, there did not seem to be anything wrong with Buster.

"Who?" said Jess. "Biddy?"

"Yes," said Buster. "Her." And they had to listen to more language, and to watch a great many more tears. Then Buster asked, "Mean to say you can't see nothing wrong?" He held out a big, strong arm shakily toward them. "Can't you *see* 'em?"

"See what?" said Frank.

"I don't know what they are," said Buster. "Things. Crawling all over, nipping and biting and scratching. Some of 'em stinging. And you can't see 'em?"

"No," said Frank and Jess.

"Then they're invisible," said Buster. "But they're there. I can feel 'em as well as see 'em. I can't move for 'em. Stafford and Ray and the rest has got 'em, too. They got the willies, and we all hid up for fear people see and ask us about 'em. I came here to see what you could do. But," said Buster, beginning to cry again, "if you can't see 'em, then you won't believe me. But they're true as I sit here. Honest. It's gut-splitting agony."

Somehow—probably because he was crying—Frank and Jess did believe him. They were both shocked that Biddy should do this to her own servants, and Jess thought how mean it was to make the Things invisible, so that no one would believe there was anything wrong with the gang.

"Please don't cry," she said.

"What did she do it for?" said Frank.

"Because of you," said Buster. "We was to get you and Ginger and the scum and bring you all to her when you come out of the Mill House. And you wouldn't come. So she got mad and said she'd teach us a lesson, not to dis-obey. *You* know we tried. She wouldn't listen."

"Buster," said Jess, "get this clear. We are *not* going to go to Biddy of our own accords, even to say you tried to bring us. Not if you paid us."

"I can't pay you," said Buster. "I got no money. They stopped our money for a window. That's why we had to sell ourselves. All I want is for you to get us out of it. Get that tooth back and stop us having to do what she wants. It's killing us all. Honest."

"We would if we could," said Frank.

"We've been trying," said Jess. "But we can't seem to."

"See here," said Buster. "If you do it, I'll be your friend. I'll stick up for you. All the gang will. We'll do anything you want, always. Promise. All you got to do is to get into that hut of hers when she's out and grab that tooth. She's got it there, in the middle. I'd grab it if I could, but she knows everything we do, now we sell ourselves."

This was not a comforting thought. Frank and Jess blinked and wondered if this meant Biddy knew Buster was in their potting shed talking to them. But a chance of getting the tooth back was too good to miss.

"How do we know when she's out?" said Frank. "Will you tell us?"

"Yes," said Buster. "I'll go down there and keep an offal-bloated lookout. I don't mind if the Things is invisible. It's the thought of people *seeing* 'em I can't stand."

"We'll be at the Mill House," said Jess. "Will you let us know?"

"First moment she's off," said Buster. "I'll come and tell you." Slowly, groaning and swearing, he took in his leg and began to get up. "Cor, zombie body-bits in catsup!" he said. "It's torture!" Then he grinned a little. "Meant to be, I suppose," he said. "But if you help, I'll make her pay for it. Promise."

At that moment, the window darkened. Frank and Jess looked round to see Vernon's face and Martin's pushed against the glass, staring at Buster. Jess hurried to open it.

Buster squeaked, "Keep away, can't you! You're worse than the Things. What do you keep doing?"

"Sorry," said Jess, and did her best to open the window without going too near Buster. She had almost forgotten about the Eyes.

"Secret weapon," Frank said smugly.

"You're telling me!" said Buster.

Jess got the window open. "It's all right," she told Martin and Vernon. "He's going to help us get the tooth back."

Vernon gave Buster a very unfriendly look. "Just him against me," he said. "It'd better *be* all right."

"Don't trust him an inch," said Martin.

"Cross my heart and hope to die, I mean it!" said Buster, and he began to cry again. That embarrassed Martin and Vernon. They looked at him and then at each other, and moved back from the window.

"I think he's all right," Jess told them. "Biddy's torturing them all, and he's going to tell us when she's out, so that we can take the tooth."

"What kind of torture?" asked Martin unbelievingly.

"Invisible," said Jess.

"So is my big toe invisible," said Vernon.

"So was the magic on the padlock at the back of her hut," said Frank. "And that hurt enough. You'd better believe him. It's our one chance to get that tooth."

144

"True," said Vernon. "Okay, I believe you, Buster, but no funny tricks."

"If you felt like me," said Buster, "you wouldn't be able to think of no funny tricks, even if you wanted to."

"Serve you right," said Vernon unfeelingly. "Now you know how Silas feels."

"*You* know it wasn't meant for him," said Buster.

"Buster," said Jess, "just go and watch for Biddy. *We* believe you. We're going to the Mill House now, to look for Jenny's heirloom."

"I say," said Frank. "I suppose you don't know where Biddy hid it, do you, Buster?"

"Hid what?" said Buster.

"The emerald necklace," said Jess. "After all, you've been stopping us looking for it."

"She never told us nothing," said Buster. "Not a vampire-brain sausage. I tell you, though—if I see it, I'll get it for you. Promise."

Even Martin and Vernon were impressed by this offer. They were almost polite to Buster while Frank took down the notice at last, and he and Jess hurried to get coats and join Martin and Vernon in the allotment path. It was beginning to rain when they got there. Buster cursed. They watched him climb the fence and go limping away across the allotments toward Biddy's hut.

"I still don't trust him," said Martin.

"We'll have to," said Vernon. "For that tooth."

There was a rustling in the grass by the fence. Everyone looked. Biddy's cat was running, crouching and cringing, past a row of cabbages and away after Buster.

"Her cat," said Vernon.

"It was in our garden," said Jess.

"After him," said Vernon. "I don't like that."

Nobody liked it. They all shivered and walked on through the rain in the direction of the road. They had just reached the end corner of the allotments when they heard the grass there rustling again. Vernon picked up a stone. They all crept across to the railings, ready to bombard that cat this time.

Though it does seem cruel, Jess thought. Even if it is a spy.

It was not the cat. It was Stafford Briggs. He was curled up in the long grass there, looking as miserable as Buster. His knees were in a clump of new-grown nettles, but he did not seem to notice. Nor did he look up. Perhaps he thought they could not see him.

"I say," said Jess. "Stafford."

Stafford's face came up and, seeing their four heads watching him over the railings, looked truly horrified. "Tomato-puke off!" he said. "Leave me be."

"It's all right, you know," said Frank. "The Things are invisible. No one can see them but the gang."

146

"What?" said Stafford. "Can't you see them?"

They shook their four heads.

"But," said Stafford, "I've got one sits on my nose. Can't you see that?"

"No," said Vernon. "You look all right to us. The same old ugly Stafford."

Stafford sat up, too relieved even to glare at Vernon. "Sure?"

"Certain," said Jess. "Buster's going to help us get the tooth back. Will you?"

"*Will* I!" said Stafford. "I'd do anything. We're all going crackers—corpse-stink crackers! We didn't get no lunch through it. I bet my mum's wild." That, as he said it, seemed to remind Stafford of something. "Here, any of you lot seen Kevin?"

Jess saw Martin and Vernon look at each other. "No," they said. "No," said she and Frank. "Why?"

Stafford looked miserable. "Nothing," he said. "It's okay. Only our mum'll twist my head off when I get back. Listen, if you do see Kevin, tell him it's all right and to go home, will you?"

They promised to do so, and left Stafford muttering and groaning and making up his mind to stand up. As soon as they were out of hearing, Frank asked Martin, "What was that about Kevin?"

"That's what made us so late," said Martin.

"Partly," said Vernon. "Seems he got desprit again. Anyway, he turns up at our place with a black eye and says he's got to see Silas. Wouldn't tell my mum who he was, or anything. So she asked me, and I said I couldn't remember."

"Why did you say that?" said Jess.

"He looked so scared," said Vernon. "And he'd got a load of cars and things he said he was giving to Silas. It didn't seem fair to stop him. So then they let him in to see Silas. Silas knew him all right, only he can't talk too well with his face like that, so it was okay."

"I think," said Jess soberly, "that the black eye was our fault. We gave poor Kevin away without meaning to, just before lunch. Oh, dear! We always seem to do something wrong."

"He's safe for now," said Martin. "Mrs. Wilkins was sorry for him. But we've had the Aunt, too."

"The Aunt!" said Frank. "Why?"

"On about painting," said Vernon. "Wants to give me lessons. Wants to paint Martin. Wants to ride on a broomstick—we think Biddy sent her. Wants her to keep an eye on us."

"Oh, dear!" said Jess. "And we got the cat. It does seem to tie up."

"Then," said Martin, "just as we were trying to get

away, we saw Mr. Adams, too, coming up the drive, and we couldn't face any more. We did a bunk over the orchard wall and ran all the way here."

"Biddy massing all her forces," said Frank. "Why?"

"Maybe," said Jess, "we're so hot on her trail that she's frightened. She's afraid we will find the necklace after all. And this means that no one's in the Mill House, so we can really search in peace. Just think if we get the necklace and the tooth this very afternoon!"

Eleven

Frankie and Jenny were leaning out of the Aunt's bedroom window when they reached the Mill House. Jess noticed someone had stuck brown paper over the broken pane.

"There's no one here," said Frankie.

"They've both gone out," said Jenny.

"Good," said Vernon. "Open the door, then. It's raining."

Frankie and Jenny vanished from the window and, after much clattering, they were heard opening the door.

"We started looking," Frankie said.

"You took so long," said Jenny.

Vernon sighed. "I knew you would. But it doesn't matter."

Jess explained what Biddy had done to the gang, even though they were her own servants. Neither little girl was surprised.

"She hates everyone," said Jenny calmly.

"And Buster deserves it," said Frankie.

"Well," said Jess, "not more than just enough to teach him a lesson. I hope she stops soon. What will happen to them if they're covered with Things at school?"

Frankie chuckled. Jess thought she was rather unfeeling, but then, she had not seen Buster crying and Stafford with his knees in a clump of nettles.

"Start searching," said Vernon. "Forget Buster. I still don't trust him."

They searched, and it did not go well. Vernon put his hand on a sticky wet picture, and Frank stuck that picture to the front of another picture while he was trying to help Vernon unstick. When he pulled the two pictures apart, they had got mixed. The milkman was spread all over a picture of Biddy's hut.

"Perhaps," he said, rather hopelessly, "we've invented a new kind of painting."

"Milkmonger," said Vernon. "Or Biddyman."

Then Frankie upset a paint pot, and while Jess was helping her mop it up, she knocked a tube of red paint down, which Martin trod on. Martin slid right across the room, leaving a trail like a bloodstain, and then he fell down on top of it. Most of the bloodstain got on his clothes.

"Oh, dear!" said Jess. "She'll know."

"So will my mother," said Martin.

Frankie fetched some turpentine and sponged him. Then she sponged the floor. While she did that, the others went on searching. They turned the whole room out, but there was no necklace. There was not so much as an earring.

"I don't think they're here after all," said Jenny.

"They *must* be," said Jess. "Or why did she try to stop us?"

Frank discovered he knew the answer to that. "She wouldn't stop us at the right place," he said. "That would be giving it away. She'd try to stop us *before* we got round to seeing where the right place must be—before we've searched all the wrong places."

"I think you're right," said Frankie.

"That means it's down at her hut," said Jenny.

"Not necessarily," said Martin.

"Why not?" said Vernon. "That's where I'd put it. With magic to keep off thieves."

"All the same," said Martin, "I think we ought to search the roof here, to be on the safe side. Mr. Adams stopped Frankie, so it *may* be there."

"And if Buster lets us know when Biddy's out," said Jess, "then we can look for the necklace when we get the tooth."

So they searched the roof—or rather, the boys did. It had almost stopped raining by this time, and gleams of sun lit the wetness of the roof until the slates looked a dazzling black. Jess stood down below and thought it looked as slippery as a glacier and quite as dangerous. Sure enough, Vernon began to slide, on his face, down the steep side, clawing and shouting.

"Just like me," said Frankie.

Frank leaned down to Vernon. Martin held Frank by the seat of his trousers and kept one arm round a chimney. The bricks of the chimney began to grind and give way. So did Frank's trousers. Vernon shouted to them to let go and he would search the gutters.

"We'll have to," said Martin, and tried to put the chimney straight again.

Vernon went with a rush and a slither down to the gutter, which began to creak and clank under his weight.

"It's not safe!" said Jess. "Don't you ever mend your house, Jenny?"

"No," said Jenny. "There's never any money."

Frank and Martin were both astride the roof, digging into chimneys. Frank found a bird's nest. Martin found a lot of soot. Vernon went clanking and creaking his way round the gutters, raking the insides of them with one toe, because he was spread out over the roof and did not dare let the gutter take his whole weight. As it was, it looked as if it would come loose any second. Dead leaves, black mud, and soggy paper came flopping down to the ground in bundles.

"Search that lot," Vernon called, rather breathlessly.

Jess left Frankie and Jenny to search. She was too nervous about Vernon. When he came to the corner of the house, the gutter led into a drainpipe, where it should have been safer. But the drainpipe was rusty. As soon as Vernon trod on the end of it, it came away from the wall, and most of the gutter came with it. Vernon shut his eyes and clung to the corner of the roof. Jess turned her head away. She just had to.

She found herself looking at a rainbow—a big, bright rainbow against a purple sky. It came right down into the trees beside the river.

"Oh, yes," said Jess. "The beauties of nature. I know."

It ought to have been lovely. Jess felt she ought to have been admiring it: the way the rainbow arched over the wide field and the way its colors melted into the new colors of the trees. You could see how big and grand it was, because there were two people running in the field, and it made them look tiny. But Jess could not attend, because, at that moment, with a squealing and a rending, the gutter came right away and Vernon fell off the roof.

He managed to hop clear. By the time Jess got to the corner of the house, Vernon was picking himself up from among a tumble of rusty iron. The drainpipe was leaning away from the side of the house. Vernon looked up at it.

"We wrecked this house," he said uneasily. "I think we'd better go."

"It was a wreck, anyway," Jess said.

"Now they've *got* to mend it," Frankie agreed, wiping smelly black mud off her fingers onto her apron.

Martin called down to know if Vernon was dead, but before Jess could call back, the two people running across the field came pelting up, shouting, "She's gone! She went out!"

They were Buster and Stafford, both soaking wet and both looking very much more cheerful.

"Been gone ten minutes now," said Buster. "Hurry!"

"Went like a rat up a drainpipe up the London Road," said Stafford. "You got ten minutes clear. Come on."

"London Road!" said Vernon. "I hope she's not after Silas."

"Or Kevin," said Jess.

"Get that tooth and we'll go on after her," said Buster. "I promised Stafford to look after Kevin, anyway. Who made this disemboweled mess?" The wrecked gutter and the leaning drainpipe were enough to catch Buster's attention in spite of his hurry.

"Vernon," said Jenny.

Buster looked at Vernon rather admiringly, Jess thought. Then he shouted up at the roof, "Get an ax-murdered move on, can't you!"

It was like magic. He had hardly said it when first Frank, then Martin, shot off the roof and landed in a tangle at their feet. Jess could not believe they were not hurt, but they seemed to be all right.

They untangled, and Frank said, "I didn't mean that fast, you idiot!"

"Sorry," said Martin. "The chimney broke."

Jess was horrified at all the damage, but Frankie and Jenny seemed quite unconcerned.

"They shouldn't have let it get so rotten," Frankie said.

"That'll teach them," Jenny said. "Good boys. You're dirty, though."

They *were* dirty. Frank and Martin were black with soot. Vernon was grayish white. Jess supposed it was the same dirt showing up differently.

"You can't talk, Jenny Adams," said Stafford. "Come on."

Jenny looked down at herself caked with thick black mud and did not answer. She came limping along after the others. Jess seized her oozy fingers to help her hurry, because, as soon as everyone was ready, Buster and Stafford went off at a hard run, back across the field, toward the river and the rainbow. The rainbow faded as they ran. No one had time to notice it, however, or breath for talking, until they reached the footbridge over the river.

Then Jess called out to Buster, "How are the Things?"

"Gone," Buster called back. "Went as soon as she went off."

"Good," Jess called, but she could not help feeling nervous. Biddy might have taken the Things off the gang because the gang had brought Frank and her to the hut. Still, she might only have thought they had been punished enough. Jess hoped that was the reason while she pulled Jenny across the bridge and along the path toward Biddy's hut.

The other seven boys in the gang were waiting by the heap of broken bicycles beyond Biddy's bare patch. They were very nervous. One of them shouted to them to hurry as soon as they were in sight.

"We'll keep guard," said Buster. "You go on in and get it."

It was plain that nothing would possess the gang to go into the hut. Frank looked at it, across the wall of petrol drums. It seemed harmless and broken enough. The cockerel was sitting on the roof. The door seemed to be half open. Getting the tooth seemed the easiest thing on earth, except that Frank had a feeling that it all seemed too good to be true. Vernon felt the same.

"You swear she really *is* out?" he said to Buster.

Not only Buster but the whole gang swore—in both senses—that Biddy had gone out. Ray Briggs and Squeaky Voice had trailed her most of the way to the London Road.

"All right," said Vernon. Then he looked at Frank. "All go in?" he asked.

Frank nearly said no. Then he remembered the Eyes, their secret weapon. "Jess and I'll go with you," he said.

"So will I," said Martin.

"And we're going," said Jenny, "because we think the necklace is in there."

So the six of them went bravely in between the petrol drums, while the gang, with an expert mutter or two, spread out round the hut and along the riverbank to keep watch. The bare patch was the same as before, except that it was not quite so airless. The rain had given it a fresher smell, for which they were all glad. Just as before, the black hens scrambled away to their hutch. And, also just as before, the cat ran across the space, crouching and cringing.

Vernon and Martin both stamped and shouted to frighten the cat away. Jess thought it was rather cruel of them, but she could see they did it because they were frightened themselves. The cat did not waste time understanding the boys. It bolted for its life, over the wall of drums and off along the riverbank. As soon as it was gone, they went to the half-open door of the hut and tried to get in.

The door was too broken to shut properly. Nor would it open easily. Frank and Martin had to take hold of it and heave it up on its rusty hinges. Then it opened. And nothing happened. No witchcraft seemed to stop them. They all crowded through, into a tiny, dirty, fuggy, dark room which smelled worse than the whole waste patch rolled into one small space.

"Pooh!" said Martin.

There were cobwebs and cobwebs, and boxes round the walls. There was a tiny, filthy window, through which they could see Stafford watching anxiously. Jess wondered where Biddy slept. There was no sign of a bed. But it was only a passing wonder because on a box in the middle of the hut was what they were looking for. There was a dirty old teacup on the box, full of strange purple fire which made a whispering noise as it leaped and licked in a neat pointed shape. It was neat and pointed except for the end of the flame, which was split into two, like a forked tongue. Over the cup, there was a thread hanging from the ceiling, and tied to the end of the thread was a small white thing, arranged to dangle between the two prongs of flame.

"That's it!" said Frank.

Vernon made a dash for it. He put his hand right into the flame, snatched at the tooth, and pulled.

And the thread would not break. It looked just like cotton, the way it draped over Vernon's hand as he pulled it clear of the forked flame, but it must have been as strong as steel. Vernon could not seem to break it. He tried frantically and, as he tried, he said things he must have learned from Buster, and his face went a strange color.

"It hurts!" he said.

"Like the lock," said Martin. "Let it go."

"I can't!" said Vernon, and to their horror, tears came pouring down his face.

"Quick, Frank!" said Jess. "The Eyes. You get the other side of him."

They both dived for Vernon. Frank, as he dived, kicked the box by mistake. The teacup fell over on its side, but it went on burning just the same, in a forked cone, and did not seem to set fire to the box. Jess put one hand on Vernon's arm and took hold of the thread with the other. As soon as she touched it, she knew why Vernon had used those words. It was like holding a red-hot poker.

"Better," said Vernon. "I still can't let go."

"*Frank!*" shouted Jess. "Help me break this thread!"

Frank put his hand on the thread, too—and yelled. They began a mad and muddled struggle, with Jess, Frank, and Vernon all trying to break the thread one-handed, and the Piries trying at the same time to keep hold of Vernon in case the Eyes helped him. After a moment, Martin took hold of Vernon, too, by his waist, and tugged. It seemed to hurt him also, through Vernon. He said a bad word as well. And, as he said it, all four of them realized that they could not let go.

"Shall we pull, too?" offered Frankie.

"No!" snapped Jess. "Don't you dare! Hunt for the necklace."

Frankie and Jenny, although they looked both hurt and alarmed, began obediently to turn out the boxes round the walls of the hut.

"What shall we *do*?" said Frank.

161

"Go backward," said Martin, without taking his teeth apart. "Pull. Get it loose if we have to have the roof down."

"Right," said Jess, and they all heaved, towing Vernon, who did not seem to be able to do anything. They went back a step, and they went back another. Then they went back three steps, in a rush, and still the thread was fastened to the ceiling, and they were fastened to the thread.

"One more," said Martin. "Now—*heave!*"

They heaved with all their strength. The thread snapped with a *twang* that sent them backward again with another rush. They had staggered ten steps before they could stop. Each step, they expected to hit the wall of the hut and, each step, there was nothing behind them at all. It was not until they had managed to stop that they looked round to find themselves in a space as vast as an airplane hangar, full of gray light and shuffling echoes. Some of the echoes were the footsteps of Frankie and Jenny, who came rushing toward them with their eyes huge with fright.

"What's happened?" said Jenny. "Why has it gone big?"

Other people were shouting the same thing. They saw

Stafford and Buster running up from another direction, looking as frightened as the little girls. The rest of the gang were blundering about behind them, and Squeaky Voice was screaming.

"Christmas!" said Martin. "I think we've all bought it."

Twelve

There was a time when everybody was shouting and talking at once.

"How the curried vampires did we get in here?" Stafford kept saying to Jess. "We was outside. I tell you, we was outside."

"There ain't no door!" shouted several other people.

"I swear it ain't got nothing to do with us," Buster said.

"Safety device," Frank said to Martin. "Built into the magic."

"Yes," said Martin. "Break one spell, and we set another going."

"It's a trap, I tell you! It's a sliming trap!" said Ray.

Jess was half deafened by the noise and by the way everyone's voices echoed. She said nothing at all and kept hold of Vernon, who was also saying nothing.

"He all right?" said Buster, looking at Vernon.

Vernon was a better color, but he seemed to be dazed. He held out his hand, which was still curled round the tooth. "It doesn't hurt," he said. "It's sort of numb. But I still can't let go."

"Good," said Jenny. "Then Biddy can't get it."

Vernon did not answer, although he tried to smile. Jess suspected he was wondering what would happen if he never could let go, and had to hold the tooth in his right hand forever. It would be like being a cripple. It was not a nice thought.

"Shall we have a go pulling his hand open?" Buster offered.

"Later," said Vernon. "Let's try to get out first."

This raised a wail from the rest of the gang. "There ain't no door!"

"There's walls, though," said Vernon. "And there's crowds of us."

"Yes," said Martin. "Let's try rushing at the walls. Come on, everyone. Charge."

"Charge!" shouted the gang. "*Charge!*" screamed Frankie and Jenny. Everyone set out at a run toward the nearest huge wall, yelling and stamping like savages. Fifteen people, even if some of them were small, would surely be able to burst out of a place like this, whatever it was.

They ran and they shouted. Then they left off shouting and just ran. After a while, they became too breathless to run, and they trotted. The trot slowed to a walk, and the walk to standing still. They stood in a scared and panting crowd and looked at the nearest wall. It was as far away as ever. For all the good their running had done, they might not have started.

"This is *silly!*" said Jess.

"You got to remember," Stafford said, "she's a maggot-gutting witch."

Jenny burst into tears. So did the smaller boys in the gang. Ray sniffed. Martin's face twisted into lumps and all his freckles showed. Jess found her eyes were hot and prickly. It was frightening to see what a strong witch Biddy must be.

"I say," Frank whispered to her, "these Eyes don't seem to do much good, do they?"

"No," Jess said miserably. "They don't." As far as she

166

could see, the Eyes did not even stop the gang coming near them now. But then, she thought, that was probably because the gang was not evil anymore. They were just nine damp, dirty, scared boys. Buster was able to come right up beside her.

"What'll we do now?" he said.

"Heaven only knows," said Jess.

"Let's sit down, anyway," said Martin. "Let's not give in."

With a great deal of shuffling and thumping, everyone sat down cross-legged in a ring. Jess found Frankie and Jenny one on each side of her. She put an arm around each of them and did, almost, feel as if she was their big sister. It was comfortable like that, even though there were great echoing spaces all round them. Everyone in the circle pressed up against the people next to them and felt cheered by feeling they were not alone.

"But," said Buster, "what'll we do when she comes? She's zombie-juiced well caught us, ain't she?"

"Not give in," Martin said again. "She may be a jolly strong witch, but that's no reason why she should have it all her own way. She's got no right to keep us here, has she? If she keeps us here very long, our parents are going to start looking for us, and then they'll find out what she's like. So I vote we keep cheerful and don't let her frighten us. Stand up to her. After all, we're fifteen to one."

"Cheek her, you mean?" said Frank.

"We mustn't make her angry," said Jess. "Every time we make her angry, she does something worse."

"I didn't mean make her angry, actually," said Martin. "I just meant not be frightened. Maybe we can think of some way to get round her."

"Yes," said Stafford. "You Piries better think of some way to get round her. Us lot'll back you up."

"Back 'em up!" said Buster dejectedly. "Like bowel pancakes we do! The moment Biddy gets here, she'll have us lot her servants again. What can we *do*?"

"No, she won't," said Vernon. "I got the tooth. You're my servants now."

Perhaps it was the way he said it, or perhaps it was just the idea, but as soon as Vernon spoke, everyone burst out laughing. The echoes took the laughter up, until the whole huge space was filled with laughing. And, when the echoes died down, everyone was in much better spirits.

"Down with Biddy!" said Jess. "Three cheers for us!"

"Let's sing," suggested Jenny.

Ray and Squeaky Voice began:

> "Old Biddy is a funny 'un
> With a face like a pickled onion—"

Before they could get any farther, the echoes boomed, and Biddy herself came hurrying up to them in great swooping strides, very much out of breath and even more out of temper.

"I have had about enough of you children," she said. "How dare you keep interfering like this! First you poke your noses in where you're not wanted, and now you burgle my house. I'll have you know you've interrupted me in something very important indeed."

"We're sorry," said Martin, perhaps not as politely as he could.

"Sorry be blowed!" said Biddy. "And I have to come running back to deal with you instead. You're very naughty little boys and girls!" She ran all round outside their circle, swooping and puffing, flapping her plimsolls on the ground, shaking her skinny plaits and peering through her thick glasses. Everyone found her frightening, but they found her rather silly, too.

Somebody gave out a whisper, "Nose like a squashed tomato!" Everyone giggled.

"That will do!" said Biddy. "I can see I shall have to teach you a lesson—all of you. Why are there so many of you? You'd think all the brats in town had broken into my hut. Which is which?"

Quite suddenly, Biddy hopped over the heads of Ray and Squeaky Voice and arrived in the middle of their ring. Everybody moved back a little. Biddy chuckled.

"You must have got your charms wrong, if you were trying for an enchanted circle," she said. "Here I am, you see." She began peering round at their faces, muttering: "Who have we got? Who have we here?" until she had picked out Frank and Jess. "You," she said. "I gave you two a clear warning not to steal my business. Own Back indeed! Don't you realize that's witch's business, not yours?"

"Yes. That's why we've given it up," said Jess.

"Given it up!" said Biddy. "You're still meddling."

"Because we're putting it right," said Frank.

"I'll put *you* right, my lad," said Biddy. "You'll be lucky to get out of here alive, all of you. As for you—" Biddy pounced round on Buster, who moved back rather quickly. "As for you, you great blubbering bully, you've hardly been my servant three days before you're whining to get out of it. Don't you have any stuffing, boy? I've a good mind to set you emptying the river with a teaspoon, just to show you who's your mistress."

"You try it," said Buster. "You just try it! You've not got the disemboweled tooth."

Biddy put her hands on her hips. "We'll see about

that," she said. Then she swung around and came swooping down on Vernon. For a moment, she peered at him through her glasses. Vernon stared back at her. Then, slowly, Biddy reached up and took off her glasses. She looked quite different without them: all shriveled, mean, and snakelike. Things were suddenly very much more frightening.

Frankie squeaked, "She did that to Jenny. Stop her!"

"Please, Miss Iremonger," said Jess, "let us go. Please. We haven't done any harm. Go back to your important business and we won't say a word."

Biddy took no notice. She stared at Vernon with her new beady snake's eyes. "Move your hand, boy," she said. They saw Vernon's hand—the one that held the tooth— twitch, and its fingers move a little. Vernon looked panic-stricken. "That's right," said Biddy. "Good boy. Now open your hand and give me that tooth."

Vernon's fingers twitched once more. His hand came up and went down again. They saw his fingers opening as if he could not stop them.

"Don't!" shouted Stafford. "Stop that, Vernon!"

Vernon clapped his left hand over his uncurling fingers and held them down. "No," he said. "I won't. You're not having it."

"Do as you're told!" snapped Biddy, and went on staring at him, twiddling her thick glasses under her chin. Vernon seemed to have to fight with himself. His left hand could not hold his right hand down. Whatever he did, his right hand came open and tried to pass the tooth to Biddy.

"Don't!" wailed Stafford and Ray.

"Can't you see he can't stop it?" said Martin, and got up on his knees to help.

Vernon's hand came up toward Biddy with the tooth in its pink palm. Biddy put out her fat mauve fingers for it.

"Bung it here, Vernon!" shouted Buster.

Vernon shut his eyes and managed to jerk his hand. The tooth shot away sideways. Buster dived for it and Biddy dived for Buster. Buster got the tooth, and before Biddy could stop him, he passed it to Ray. Ray at once tossed it to Stafford. Everyone knelt up and closed in, shrieking, as if it were a mad game of Pass the Parcel. Biddy ran round and round the circle, shouting that they were naughty children. They all shouted back, and fumbled and rolled and waved their hands, so that she should not see who had the tooth. It went from person to person. Frank had it. He gave it to Martin. Martin put it in Frankie's hand and Frankie clapped it in Jess's. Biddy pounced round, and Jess threw it into Jenny's lap.

"I got it!" screamed Squeaky Voice, on the other side of the circle. "Here, Ray!"

Biddy was fooled and dived at them. Ray pretended to pass it to Stafford, and Stafford held out his empty hands to show her she was fooled.

"That will do!" said Biddy. "Sit still, all of you."

Somehow, they all found they had to sit still.

"That's better," said Biddy. "Don't move."

Nobody moved. Nobody could. They sat cross-legged in a ring, like the most obedient class at school. Biddy looked all round them with her uncovered piercing eyes.

"Own up, the one who has the tooth," she said.

Nobody answered. Nobody gave a sign. Jess wondered who had it by now. Whoever he was, he was not giving it away. Everyone looked defiant, but nobody looked guilty.

"Very well," said Biddy. "You can stay like that and see how you like it. Perhaps, when I come back, you'll be ready to tell me." Saying this, she hopped over their heads again and went shuffling away into the vast space, leaving them all sitting in a ring, quite unable to move.

"Mean slime-drooling trick!" said Buster.

"The one who's got it mustn't tell us," said Jess. "We might give it away if we know."

They sat there for ages. They sat for what seemed to

be hours. They sat until they were so uncomfortable that they all wanted to scream. The worst of it was that, although they could not move, they were not numb like Vernon's hand. They felt things in the usual way. The floor had been hard to start with, and it got harder and harder. Their legs ached with being crossed. Their arms had pins and needles. Their necks hurt with having to stay in one position. They were so uncomfortable that they became crosser and crosser. The gang quarreled among themselves and jeered at the others.

"Shut up," said Frank. "It was you lot wanted the tooth in the first place."

"And who was it got it for us?" said Buster.

"Me," said Vernon. "And you ought to see Silas."

"I say," said Jess. "Do you think he's better now?"

"He should be," said Martin. "We must have broken the spell, surely."

That seemed to cheer everyone up, until they remembered that Biddy had been up the London Road. Everyone was sure she had gone to the big house to see Silas. Frankie suggested singing again, but no one had the heart even to start. They sat without talking for another age, until Jess noticed that Biddy had come back. Half the circle could not see her, because she was behind them, but Jess had a clear view of her.

Biddy was sitting outside the circle in a cane chair. There was a table beside her with plates on it, as if she had just finished supper. Biddy was leaning back, smoking a cigar and taking no notice of the children. None of them noticed she was there, except Jess, until the cat jumped up on the table and tried to lick one of the plates.

Biddy knocked the cat on to the floor. "Get down," she said to it. "I told you no supper and no breakfast, and I meant it. You were supposed to tell me what these brats were up to. Instead, you let them plot and plan and break into the hut. Get away. I'm very cross with you."

She tried to kick the cat. It backed away and spat at her plimsoll. Jess did not blame it. She watched the cat, looking very ruffled and angry, creep under the table and pretend to wash itself. She felt as angry as it looked. As soon as Biddy talked of supper, Jess had realized that she was terribly hungry. So had everyone else.

"I'm sorry I threw those spoons," said Frank. "I know just how it feels."

"Be quiet," said Biddy.

"We'll talk if we want to," said Martin. "You were saying, Frank?"

"I was saying," said Frank, "that Christmas is coming and the geese—"

"Hot cross buns," said Vernon.

"Steak and kidney pudding, you mean," said Buster.

"Disemboweled fish and chips," answered Stafford.

"Pancakes," said Jenny, "and I like mine with syrup, but Frankie likes—"

"Oh, don't!" said Frankie. "Jess, can't you and Frank think of something? This is awful!"

Jess made a face. It was a hard thing when everyone was relying on them to have good ideas. She was too hungry to think. Yet then, she thought, the sight of the cat sitting crossly under the table had given her some sort of idea, if only she could think what it was—if only the rest of them would stop talking about food!

"Strawberries and cream," said Martin.

"No, tinned zombie-bits peaches."

"Anything!" said Jess. The idea had gone.

Biddy chuckled, very cheerfully. They all hated her. "Well," she said. "Now perhaps the person who has the tooth will own up."

"Can we," asked Buster longingly, "can we all go as soon as they done it?"

"Good gracious, no!" said Biddy. "What gave you that idea? You nine are my servants and I happen to need you urgently."

"We're not your degutted servants," said Buster.

"Whose are you, then?" laughed Biddy.

"The one that has the tooth's, of course," Buster said.

"Then," said Biddy, "the one that has the tooth had better say so. They can have the pleasure of giving you my orders."

No one answered, until Jess said, "The one that has the tooth—can *they* go home when they've given the orders?"

"What do you think I am?" said Biddy. "Naturally not. I need the tooth. I need my servants, and I need to make sure you don't tell naughty tales. None of you is going home."

There was a very miserable silence. Then Martin said, "But you *can't*. Our parents will come looking for us. They're bound to find us in the end."

"Why should they find you?" Biddy asked. "You're in my private house here. No one can find that except me. They may search the hut as they please—they won't find so much as a whisker of you."

Whisker! Jess thought. Why is whisker important? Why is the cat important?

"So," said Biddy, "you might as well give me the tooth. I'll get it in the end, anyway."

Nobody answered. Biddy waited for a while. Then she seemed to give the tooth up for the present.

"We'll come to the really urgent matter," she said. "Frances Adams, you may as well own up. Why has your father gone to your old house—Martin Taylor's house?"

"I don't know," said Frankie. "Because you told him to, I suppose."

"I did not," said Biddy. "I forbade him to go. I ordered him off, and he disobeyed me. I want you to tell me why."

"I don't know why," said Frankie. "And even if I did, I wouldn't tell, because you made Jenny's foot bad."

"She never did!" said Stafford, sounding really shocked.

"She did," said Jenny.

"Anyway," said Buster to Biddy, "why shouldn't her father go up there? You don't gizzard well own him."

"Yes, I do," said Biddy. "*And* her aunt. I own the whole family now, don't I, Frances?"

"No," said Frankie.

"I do now," said Biddy. "Or I will soon, my dear. I have your heirlooms and your jewelry, and half your money, too. I've turned you out of your house, and I won't stop until the lot of you are squashed beneath my feet like wood lice. There you have it."

"Why?" said at least six people. "That's sliming horrible. Why?"

"Ah," said Biddy, "to teach him a lesson—my dear Mr. Adams. He could have married me, and he married a fluffy girl instead. I sent her away. I'll show him what he's missed."

Everyone was by now so cross and so uncomfortable and so sick of Biddy that they answered her with roars of laughter.

"Cor!" said Buster. "Marry *you!* Who d' you think you are? Lady Godiva?"

"You're wicked," said Jess and Jenny.

"She's mad," said Frank and Frankie.

"Biddy the Bride! Twice round the gut-slimed gas-works!" yelled the gang.

"I bet he never even looked at her," said Martin to Vernon, and Vernon agreed.

Biddy was very annoyed. "I've had enough of this," she said, whipping off her glasses again. "Be quiet. Be quiet, all of you."

Everyone was quiet. Not one of them could speak.

"So there!" said Biddy. "Now I'll have to go and see if the wretched man is home yet." She stood up and began shuffling away again. The cat crawled out from under the table and tried to make friends by rubbing round her mauve legs. Biddy kicked it away and shuffled off.

She left the fifteen children all rolling their eyes at one another helplessly. There was a long, long silence. Then Frank said, "Can't anybody really talk?"

"Yes," said Jess. "But I can't move."

She could see from the rolling eyes of the others that

they could not talk and were amazed that she and Frank still could.

"Why can we talk?" said Frank.

"The Eyes," said Jess. "They must still be working a bit."

"That's a relief," said Frank. "Do you think that's why she couldn't find which one had the tooth?"

"I hope so," said Jess. "Have you got it? I haven't."

"No," said Frank. "And it's lucky the one who has can't talk. Don't ask. She mustn't get it. If we know, we might give it away. What can we do, Jess?"

"Think of an idea," said Jess. "Some way to get round her."

"I can't," said Frank. "Not when she's chuckling and saying what she's done to the Adams family. She just makes me sick—even though I'm so hungry I could eat my fingers if I could move them."

"So is the cat hungry," said Jess. "Does that help?"

"I could eat *it*," said Frank. "It had better not come too near me."

Jess rolled her eyes round and saw the cat on the table, despairingly licking the empty plates. "Lucky thing!" she said. "Gravy, at least."

After that, they sat in hopeless silence for a long, long time. Frank thought that, uncomfortable though they were, they dropped off to sleep for a while. He remembered seeing Buster's eyes closed, and Jenny's. He started noticing things again when somebody began snoring.

Whoever it was snored great rattling snores that went through Frank's head like someone drilling a tooth. He looked, and saw that Biddy was back again. She had tipped her chair back and turned it into a sort of bed. Her mouth was open, her glasses were off, and she looked dreadful. The cat was sitting on the table staring at her spitefully. It looked as if it hated Biddy quite as much as Frank did.

"I agree with you," Frank said, and the cat flipped the end of its tail at him. "I agree with you so much," said Frank, "that I'm sorry I threw those spoons at you." The cat flipped its tail again but took no other notice.

"Frank," said Jess.

"What?" said Frank. The snoring and the talking had roused the others. Their eyes were open all round the circle, and he thought how miserable they all looked. "Get an idea," he said to Jess. "For goodness' sake."

"I have," said Jess. "At last. 'Puss in Boots.'"

"It isn't," said Frank. "It hasn't even got shoes on."

"Don't be a stupid idiot," said Jess. "And I can't say too much. Just remember the end of the story."

Frank thought. He remembered, and he saw the idea.

He saw, from the way Vernon's eyes rolled and Frankie's, that they had seen the idea, too. They all looked at the snoring Biddy and were afraid in case she had heard Jess in her sleep. But Biddy snored on.

"Will it work?" said Frank.

"We can try," said Jess. "Maybe the Eyes will help. Let's ask the cat."

"Does it understand?"

"It *must* do, the way she talked to it. Let's try, anyway."

"Okay," said Frank. "I say. Cat." Biddy gave a rattling snore and stirred a little.

"Not so loud!" said Jess.

Frank tried again, in a loud whisper. "Cat. I say." The cat looked round at him. As soon as it was looking at him, Frank felt very foolish indeed. It was only an animal. It could not possibly understand. "Do you know the end of 'Puss in Boots'?" he said to it hopelessly. The cat blinked. It did not look in the least as if it understood. "Bother you, then," said Frank.

"It doesn't matter," Jess said quickly. "Listen, cat, you're cross with Biddy, aren't you, for not giving you any supper?" The cat did not move, except for the end of its tail, which swished quickly backward and forward. "We'll give you supper," said Jess, "if you do what we tell you.

Will you?" The cat just went on swishing its tail and staring at her. "You try, Frank," said Jess.

"Cat," said Frank. "Go and wake Biddy up. Then we'll show you."

The cat shut its eyes. It seemed that there had been no point in talking to it after all. Then it opened its eyes, got onto its four feet, and stretched. If it was going to help them, it was plainly going to do it as if it was its own idea, not theirs. Slowly, yawning, it walked among the plates on the table. Then it sat down again. Frank and Jess gave it up. Then, when they were quite hopeless, it suddenly jumped on Biddy, right in the middle of her chest. Then it jumped off again, fast. Biddy woke up and hit out at it, but it was under the table by then, growling.

"Dratted animal!" said Biddy. She stretched, and they saw her look round to see if the children were awake. "Little dears," she said. "What a lovely night you must have had! I hope you ache all over. Now—" Biddy stretched again and seemed to be thinking. "The question is what to do with you," she said. "I can't have you sitting about forever. It's a nuisance. Why is it so difficult to turn live things into things which aren't alive? I wish I could turn you all into a ring of tin cans. But it would take too long, and I want you safely out of the way before the police start asking awkward questions. It'll have to be toads, I suppose. No. Because then you'll all go hopping off, and I want you where I can make you miserable. I know! Grass! I'll turn you into fifteen grass roots and plant you where you'll get walked on. That's it!"

Biddy got up quickly, as if she was pleased with this idea. Jess swallowed and said, "Miss Iremonger."

Biddy shot a beady look at her. "What are you doing, wagging your tongue?" she said. "You're not supposed to."

"I know," said Jess. "But I want to know if you can do real magic."

"Real magic!" said Biddy. "What do you think I've been doing all this time, if it's not real magic?"

"No," said Jess. "It isn't."

"She means, can you turn things into other things," said Frank.

"That's *real* magic," said Jess.

"Is it?" said Biddy. "Strange ideas you do have. Didn't you hear me just now, Jessica Pirie? What do you think I was talking about? The man in the moon?"

"Yes, I heard you," said Jess. "But I wanted to see you *do* it. I don't believe you really can."

Biddy rubbed her chin and shuffled a few steps toward Jess. "Don't you, my dear?" she said. "Well, it's quite simple. I'll turn you into a toad now, if you like—unless you'd rather be a dandelion."

Jess could think of nothing to say, because her idea seemed to have gone wrong. She wondered if the cat ate toads. "Dandelion, please," she said, just to be on the safe side.

"No," said Frank. "Don't do it to her. Do it to yourself, Miss Iremonger. Turn *yourself* into something."

Biddy shuffled at him. "And why should I do that, Master Pirie? I'm not a television show, you know. Why should I go to the trouble for you?"

Frank could not think of a reason, except the right one.

But he could not have Jess turned into a dandelion, so he began to talk hard, hoping a reason would come to him.

"Well," he said, "if you do it to her, *I* can see her, but she can't, can she? If you turn her into a dandelion, she might not know she was one, even if we told her. She wouldn't have ears and eyes and things. It would be the same for all of us. So when you turn us into grass and plant us, we might not know we really *were* grass, and we wouldn't believe it when people walked on us. And," said Frank desperately, "that wouldn't be nearly such fun for you, would it?"

Biddy rubbed her chin. "You've a good head, Master Pirie. You have a point there. I never thought of that."

"But," said Frank cunningly, "if you were to turn *your-self* into something, Miss Iremonger, we could all see it and believe it."

Perhaps he had been too cunning. Biddy said, "And where do you think that would get you? Are you playing some game, Master Pirie?"

Frank could not answer.

"Frank," said Jess. "I knew it! She can't really! She doesn't know how to. There's no need for us to worry."

"Oh, isn't there?" said Biddy. "You just watch, Miss Pirie." She put her arms out and looked to make sure they were watching. "Now," she said. "What shall it be? Shall I be a nice brown cow? Or a mad bull?"

"Not a cow," said Frank. "That's too near what you are." He had not meant to be rude, but he saw Vernon's face and Martin's and Buster's twitching, as if they would laugh if they could.

"An elephant," said Jess hurriedly. "Be a great huge elephant, Miss Iremonger."

"Very well," said Biddy. "Here goes." She stretched her arms out straighter and began to mutter. The muttering became louder, and louder, until the echoes were filled with it, and Biddy's voice was roaring and trumpeting all round the huge space. She began to swell and grow gray. Her front teeth grew into tusks, and her plaits spread out and became ears. Her nose shot out into a trunk—and, the next second, there was an enormous, trampling elephant.

Its face was like Biddy's. The little reddened eyes were the same, all mean and sharp; and, perhaps because its features were now so big, its face seemed twenty times more unpleasant than Biddy's own. And it had still not finished changing. It grew larger yet. Rough black hair sprouted on its back and shoulders. Its tusks grew longer and ever more pointed, until they seemed as sharp as sickles, and its face became every second more ferocious. At length, it was a thing like a mammoth, which stood shifting its heavy feet outside the circle of children.

Jess saw the cat under the table with its hair on end and its back arched, staring at the elephant. Oh, dear! she thought. I hope it doesn't run away.

Biddy turned her trunk toward Frank and trumpeted, in a great huge voice that sounded as if she were holding her nose, "There! Are you satisfied now, Master Pirie?"

Frank's teeth were chattering. He had known Biddy was evil, but he had not realized how much. In this form, he felt you simply could not trust her, and she terrified him. "Splendid!" he shouted above the echoes. "Show everyone."

The Biddy elephant nodded and went off on a trample round the ring of children, making as she went vicious sideways swings of her tusks that just missed their helpless backs. They rolled their eyes at her, and most of them went pale. Frank, though he had never felt less like admiring anything, pretended to be pleased.

"Isn't she lovely?" he shouted to Jess.

Jess shouted back through the noise of Biddy's trampling, "Yes, but that's too easy. I bet she can't do something small."

"Oh, you bet, do you?" boomed the elephant. "How much?"

"Fifty pence!" shouted Frank.

"Fifty pence to be what?" boomed Biddy.

Jess pretended to think. "Something little," she said. "Like a—like a *mouse!*"

"*Done!*" bawled Biddy. The elephant immediately began to shrink and lose its shape. By the time it was the size of a horse it was a smooth gray thing on four legs, though it still had small tusks. When it was the size of a dog, it had lost its tusks and its legs seemed to be bending in underneath it somehow. Still it shrank and dwindled, until all either Frank or Jess could see was a writhing gray blob. Then they lost sight of the blob. There came a tiny scuttering, which made the cat prick up its ears.

A little gray mouse came running between Jenny and Jess and out into the middle of the circle. There it sat up

188

on its haunches and squeaked in a small sharp voice, "Here we are again, my dears. How's that? Have I won my bet?"

Jess looked at the cat. Its eyes were huge, yellow and intense. It was crouching down. Its tail was slashing from side to side, and it was rocking on its back legs, ready to spring.

"Well?" squeaked the mouse, rather crossly. "Don't you believe me? Have I won my bet?"

"I believe you," said Frank.

The cat stared, but still it did not pounce. Jess saw that they would have to make Biddy run about before the cat would move.

"Are you a real mouse?" she called out. "Can you run?"

The mouse at once put its forepaws to the ground and ran toward her in irregular swoops, just like Biddy usually walked. "Of course I'm a real mouse!" it snapped. The cat lashed its tail and stared, but still it did not spring. The mouse glared spitefully up at Jess, and Jess thought it the most unpleasant-looking creature she had ever seen. Its snout was long and vicious. All the ferocity of the elephant seemed to have got packed and concentrated into its one small face. She shuddered.

"Can you nibble, too?" asked Frank. He hoped Biddy would run over to him, but she simply cocked her head his way.

"Nibble?" she squeaked. "I have extremely sharp teeth, Master Pirie. Shall I chew your knee as a demonstration?"

"If you like," Frank said bravely.

"No," said Jess. "Chew Buster's." Buster rolled his eyes at her indignantly, and Jess made a face to show him it could not be helped. Buster was now the one farthest away from the mouse, and they just had to make it run right across the circle somehow.

"Buster's knee?" said the mouse. "With pleasure." It turned and darted, swooping and snaky, straight for Buster. Jess gasped. Frank watched the cat. The cat gathered up its back legs and—

They never saw it move. It went too fast. One moment it was under the table, the next it was a blur, and the next moment it was on the mouse. There was a Biddy squeak, a mouse squeak, and a sort of crunching.

As soon as they heard the crunch, there was a jolt. The next thing they knew, all fifteen children were shouting and crammed together into the tiny space inside Biddy's hut.

Thirteen

"Talk about *brains*!" Buster said admiringly.

"Get off my foot," said Vernon to Stafford.

The hut was far too small to hold them all. It was creaking, giving at the joints. Before anyone was clear what had happened, one of the side walls gave way completely. It swung out from the roof and fell with a slap on the ground, like a big door opening. They were all dazzled by bright sunlight. The cat ran from among their legs with the mouse in its mouth, over the fallen wall, and out.

Jess, feeling terribly stiff, pushed Frankie aside and

limped out after it. Everyone streamed after her into a red-and-gold wet morning. The cat, seeing them, ran up the nearest big willow tree. All they could do was to stand staring up at it, as it scrambled from branch to green-gold branch, with the mouse dangling like a bundle of old string from its mouth.

"I'm afraid it's gone," said Jess.

"Good riddance!" said Martin.

No one bothered with the cat anymore, because the hut collapsed then. First the roof fell in. The black hens and the cockerel rushed out of their petrol drum and ran squawking and flapping away along the riverbank. Then the double door at the back of the hut toppled into the river. The two walls left fell on top of the roof, knocking down the petrol drums on the way. All that was left was a heap of rotten wood only fit for a bonfire. Someone, in fact, suggested setting fire to it, but Buster said it was too damp to burn.

"I suppose," said Frankie, staring at it, "I suppose it was only held together by magic."

"Pretty rotten magic, then," said Frank.

"But you and Jess broke the spell," Frankie said.

"Or the cat did," said Jess.

Jenny limped up to Vernon. "Here you are," she said. "I just had time to put it in my pocket before she looked."

She put her hand in her apron pocket and brought out the tooth. Vernon, grinning all over his face, took the tooth and put it in his own pocket.

"Thanks," he said.

"It was you, Jenny Adams!" said Ray admiringly. "And you never let on one bit! Like a real good 'un."

Jenny went very pink. Looking all pretty and pleased, she went over and took Frankie's hand.

"Isn't it a shame!" Jess said to Frank. "She's still limping. We never found the necklace after all."

Vernon heard and came over to Jess. "Let's look now," he said. "I bet anything it's here." Jess saw him look round, toward the hut. Before she could agree, Vernon's eyes grew big and white all round like bull's eyes. He gave a scream of excitement and set off running for the heap of rusty bicycles beside the path. Jess tore after him. She was in time to see him snatch the nearest bicycle chain away and hold it up. As he held it up, it flashed all long and bright, like the green stripe in a rainbow.

"Jenny!" yelled Vernon.

Jenny pattered up, as white as she had been pink before.

"This it?" said Vernon, and Jenny nodded. "Fair exchange," said Vernon, and passed the necklace over. Jenny held it in both hands, and her hands wobbled.

"Try walking," said Vernon. "Go on."

Everyone stood round while Jenny took a few steps. At first, there seemed to be no difference, but, as Jess said afterward, that must have been because Jenny was so nervous that she could not walk straight. In six steps she was walking properly, with both feet firmly planted. They all cheered. Jenny jumped up and down, bright pink again.

"Put it round your neck," said Stafford. "Not to lose it."

So Jenny put the emerald necklace on, and everyone turned to Vernon, shouting to know how he had found it.

"Out of the corner of my eye," said Vernon. "I saw it shine. When I looked straight on, it was a rusty chain again." He was very excited. "There was more, wasn't there?" he said to Frankie.

Frankie nodded. "All sorts of things."

"I bet she's got it all hidden here," said Vernon. "In the rubbish."

"Come on!" shouted Buster. "Let's look."

They began an extraordinary treasure hunt. People ran in all directions through the fresh wet grass, shouting, and pouncing on anything that shone. Frank took the chain off another bicycle, and it was a string of things like glass that shone every color under the sun. He passed it to Frankie, because it was her heirloom. He took off another chain, and it was just a chain. The rule seemed to be that you looked at something else, saw a glitter to one side, and if you picked up the glittering thing, however unlikely, it was something precious.

Buster picked up an old hubcap, and it was a silver plate. Jess, unbelievingly, took hold of a rusty kettle and found it was a bowl to match the plate. Bedsprings became candlesticks, tin cans silver cups, and wire and the works of clocks became brooches and bracelets. The loveliest thing was a necklace of little pearls, which had seemed to be barbed wire. They put everything in a heap on the path, and Stafford stood over it to keep it safe.

People made mistakes, of course. Jenny put her hand on a spiderweb covered with dew, and it was still a cobweb. Jess picked up a tin can, and it was still a tin can.

"All that glitters is not gold," she said, and threw it away. Then she saw Ray and Squeaky Voice bending over another tin can, and went to see what it was.

"Cor!" Ray was saying. "We can buy no end of stuff with this!"

Jess looked over their shoulders and found that the can was packed full of money. Before she could object, Buster came up behind her.

"Drop it!" he said. "That goes on the pile, too. It's theirs."

Then everyone began searching cans for money. They

found it in heaps. Buster was very strict. He ran about roaring threats and would not let the gang pocket so much as a halfpenny. Jess was very glad he did. What they heaped on the path seemed to them to be a small fortune.

"It must be yours," she said to Frankie and Jenny. "It's the money Biddy took. Fancy anyone being so mean!"

"At least she didn't spend it," said Frank.

They were kneeling in the path, trying to count the money, when they heard shouting from the river. Everyone looked round. There were two policemen, followed by a whole line of other people, running across the footbridge. The parents of fifteen children make an awful lot of people, Jess thought, sitting on her heels and watching them, even if some of the children are brothers and sisters. There was Mr. Taylor, and her own father, Mr. Wilkins, Mr. Adams, and a great big flat-nosed man who could only be Buster's father. And there was a whole string more, and some mothers. Jess felt rather tired at the sight of them, and a little like crying.

Then the parents swept down on them, and there was kissing and shaking and questions. "What possessed you?" "Why have you been out all night?" "Where have you all *been*?" "Buster, for two pins I'd take my belt to you!"

None of the children could do much except point to

the heap of treasure, and say, "Look what we found. It's the Adams's stuff."

"I believe it *is*, you know," said the Aunt, striding among the parents and, Jess thought, looking a good deal less vague than usual. The Aunt fetched Vernon a wallop on the back which nearly knocked Mr. Wilkins over, too. "Good for you, shadow!" she said. Frank thought Mr. Wilkins looked cross.

"Can you identify this as yours, sir?" a policeman asked Mr. Adams.

Mr. Adams, very cheerfully, pushed through beside the Aunt. He did not look vague, either. "Yes," he said. "I can. I've got the list in my desk."

"Three cheers!" said Martin. "Now they won't mind about the house."

"Why should we?" said Mr. Adams. "It was far too large for us, you know." Martin did not know how to answer.

The other policeman was looking at the ruined hut. "Any of you children know what became of Miss Iremonger?" he asked.

"The cat ate her," said Jess, and of course no one believed her. Her father told her not to make stupid jokes. Jess was nearly in tears at being scolded, when she found someone who did believe her.

It was the lady who had given her the Eyes. She came pushing through the people to Jess, and she had Frankie and Jenny hanging on to each of her arms.

"Well done, Jessica," she said. Then she winked. "'Puss in Boots'?" she said.

Jess nodded. The lady looked quite different now—very happy and young and nice.

"This is my mother," Jenny said proudly. "She's our mother."

"She came back," said Frankie. "Daddy went to fetch her, in spite of what Biddy said."

"Oh, I am glad!" said Jess.

Then, while the policemen were importantly gathering up the treasure, there was more shouting from the direction of the allotments.

"Come back, you little nuisances!" somebody shouted.

Everyone looked round and saw Kevin and Silas, running along the path as hard as they could go, with Mrs. Briggs and Mrs. Wilkins after them, as hard as *they* could go.

"Silas ought to be in bed," Mrs. Wilkins panted. "Stop him!"

Silas would not be stopped. He ran until he reached Vernon, and when he reached him, he threw his arms

round him and butted his head into Vernon's stomach. Vernon bent down to hear what he said.

"What's he saying?" asked Frank.

Vernon grinned. "Says he was coming to rescue us," he said. "They both were."

"How *brave*!" said Jenny.

Silas turned round, very shyly, and smiled. His face, Jess and Frank were relieved to see, was the right size again.

Kevin had been caught by Mr. Briggs and picked up. But he turned round and shouted down to the Piries, "You did it?"

"Yes," said Jess.

"Then I owes you five pence," Kevin said.

"Forget it," said Frank.

There is not very much more to tell, except that Frank and Jess made some money after all. Mr. Adams called the next day and gave them each two pounds.

"After all," he said, "I seem to have got my Own Back, so it's only fair you should be paid."

Jess allowed Frank to take the money this time. They had found the treasure, after all, she said, so that Mr. Adams could pay for the broken chimney and gutter. And Jess had a feeling, too, that it was she who had told Mr.

Adams that the lady called Jessica was at Martin's house. So it seemed fair. But they never could discover whether Mr. Adams understood about Biddy or not.

Nobody else could understand where Biddy had got to. Jess gave up trying to explain. She and Frank made a number of efforts to catch the cat, but it would never let anyone come near it. It continued to live on the waste patch, and every time Jess set eyes on it, it seemed to have grown fatter and sleeker. In the end they left it alone. It was obviously quite happy the way it was.

The gang spent a lot of time near the hut searching for more money and treasure. They never found much, but sometimes, other people who least expected it would come across money there and, at times, a brooch or so. No one knew whether these belonged to the Adams family, or whether they were things Biddy had taken from somewhere else, but it made the waste ground very interesting.

As for Buster, he kept his word about being friends with Piries, and with the others, too. Nobody could call him a reformed character. He still had his gang. He still used slimy and disemboweled language. But he was not so much of a bully after that. Perhaps, in some ways, he did learn a lesson. At all events, Frank and Jess, and Vernon, too, became very friendly with the whole gang.

The Aunt's picture did rather well. It got shown by an

important gallery in London, and Frank and Jess and Martin and Vernon were allowed to go up to London for the day to meet the Aunt and see the picture. Frank thought it was just as triangular and thick as before, and Martin agreed. But Jess and Vernon thought it had its points.

"We sort of crystallize out of it," Jess explained.

"Like from a lot of mirrors," said Vernon.

"Bravo!" said the Aunt.

But, to their intense disgust, the picture was called *Urchins*.

"And we're *not*!" Jess whispered, looking at them all in their best clothes.

"We were that day. A bit," said Frank.

"Scarlet all over," said the Aunt, "like Buster's language. Come on. Knickerbocker Glories all round to celebrate. And milk shakes, too, if your innards will stand it."

"Oh, they will," said Vernon earnestly.